IN WITCH THE NEW

A BLAIR WILKES MYSTERY

ELLE ADAMS

In a beat of shimmering wings, I flew past the barrier keeping the town of Fairy Falls hidden from human sight. As my dad and I emerged from the magical world into the normal one, we came to an immediate halt when I held out a hand and hissed, "Normals, up ahead."

The pair of hikers I'd spotted was too far away to see us appear out of thin air, thankfully, but we'd have to forego our wings for a bit. In unison, we snapped our fingers and conjured up glamours to hide our wings and pointed ears. The bright sheen of fairy magic that surrounded us at all times wasn't visible to most people anyway, but I was more at ease in glamour than my dad was, having worn one unknowingly for most of my life.

Dad gave me a questioning look. "How do I look?"

"Positively ordinary." My dad's silky-smooth and raven-black hair fell to his shoulders, but it no longer glowed like an advertisement for a particularly potent magical shampoo. The shirt and tie he'd chosen to wear only enhanced the impression of ordinariness. "Mr and Mrs Wilkes will think you're an important businessman who lives in a suit and tie."

Putting together a meeting between my utterly ordinary foster parents and my biological father—whom I'd only met face to face recently—was harder than one would think. While I'd successfully blended in as a regular human for the first twenty-five years of my life, the glamour my father had put on me had been for another purpose too. Namely, to prevent me from becoming a target for both of my magical parents' many enemies. I scanned the two hikers walking through the field, but they were dressed like tourists, not paranormal hunters. Good.

"That's the plan," my dad responded. "As long as they don't ask me any questions about my actual job, I might just get away with the ruse."

"Tell them you work for a top-secret department of the local government and are sworn to secrecy." The latter part was technically true, since telling non-magical folk about the paranormal world was against the rules. Yet another reason why setting up this meeting had been a challenge.

When I'd first entered the magical world myself, I'd been unaware that I'd obliviously broken the law just by wandering past the boundary to Fairy Falls. Since I'd turned out to have magic of my own, I'd been allowed to stay, but that wouldn't have been true of the couple who'd raised me while my biological dad had been locked up for a lifelong sentence in a high-security magical prison. As far as I was concerned, that was a fairly significant excuse for him not being there to welcome me to the magical world in person. But now that he was free, he was determined to make up for lost time, starting with introducing himself to the ordinary humans who'd raised me.

We passed the two hikers and made our way to the outskirts of the ordinary town of Sloan. Cars rumbled past, and mundane chatter filled the air as non-magical folk went about their daily existences, oblivious to the other realms and beings that lived alongside them.

"We fit right in here, see?" I gestured at the grey pavements and terraced houses. "Nobody is going to look twice at us."

That wasn't strictly true. For my whole life, I'd felt out of step with the rest of the world. Mr and Mrs Wilkes had done their best with me after plucking me out of the foster home and loving me as their daughter, but I seemed to stumble from one catastrophe to the next until I'd wound up in Fairy Falls and finally found myself sliding into place like a missing jigsaw piece, completing the puzzle that was my life. Since I'd always appreciate what my foster parents had done for me, I found myself longing to bridge the gap between my two lives.

Even if it meant twisting the truth a little to avoid breaking the laws. It wasn't only the legalities of the paranormal world that concerned me but the dangers too. Recently, my foster parents had had a terrifying experience involving the goblin market and its resident fairies, which had been traumatising for everyone involved. Their memories of those events had been erased, but my own memory was crystal clear, and I would do everything in my power to prevent a repeat performance.

My dad and I made our way to the shopping centre—where my foster parents had met my boyfriend, Nathan, a few months ago—and waited outside. Everything seemed grey compared to the brightness of Fairy Falls, even the part that wasn't covered in fairy glamour, but it was also a hundred percent free of magical dangers. *I hope.* I found my gaze lingering on any bright colours or sparkles and was glad we hadn't decided to meet near the jewellery shop.

"I can tell you're nervous," said Dad. "Relax, Blair. We'll be fine. Your cover story is great, and they won't be expecting any trouble."

"Last time, my cat showed up," I recalled. "Though I asked Sky if he wanted to come with us before I left the house, and he just went back to sleep, so I'm guessing that won't happen this time. Still, that's the least of what might go wrong."

My cat showing up in weird places wasn't an obvious sign that he might be anything other than an ordinary feline, so I wouldn't have to invent a cover story in that particular instance. As a fairy cat, Sky had adopted me as much as I'd adopted him. Kind of like my foster parents, in a way. I kept an eye out for them among the chattering crowd of weekend shoppers as a few raindrops began to fall on our heads.

"Better get inside," Dad suggested.

"All right."

We both ducked into the shopping centre before we got drenched in one of England's many rainstorms. Unfortunately, a lot of other people had the same idea, and the surge of movement in our direction set my nerves spiking.

"We should get a table before they're all gone."

I entered the café near the shopping centre's entrance,

my dad on my heels, and nobody looked at us twice as we picked a table near the window, where Mr and Mrs Wilkes would easily be able to spot us. After all, we looked like an ordinary father and adult daughter out together. A pang hit my chest as I wished my mother could have been here for this moment, but she'd died before I'd ever had the chance to meet her in the flesh. Nevertheless, we'd been lucky to talk when her ghost had briefly appeared on Samhain, and that would have to be enough.

Dad smiled at me, a hint of sadness in his gaze, and I wondered if the same thought had crossed his mind. "We're in a good spot to people-watch."

"Trust me, you're going to be disappointed with the level of ordinariness compared to Fairy Falls."

I probably shouldn't speak too soon, given that my last visit to this coffee shop had been interrupted by the ravings of a normal under the influence of goblin brew who'd been able to see my wings. Not to mention my cat deciding he needed to introduce himself as well. Hardly as outrageous as vampires, werewolves, shifters, fairies, and everything else that comprised the magical world, but my penchant for attracting disaster remained firmly intact.

"Sometimes ordinary is what we need," Dad said.

On the other side of the rain-specked window, I spotted a man dressed in a muddy brown coat elbowing his way through the crowd, glancing wildly around him as if he was being attacked by invisible pixies. Which he wasn't, because I would have been able to see them. Our gazes locked for a brief moment through the window, and his eyes bulged, but the crowd swallowed him up a moment later. Weird. While he'd been behaving as if he could see something that the crowd around him seemed oblivious to, that didn't necessarily mean magical involvement—you saw all sorts of weirdos hanging around shopping centres.

I turned back to Dad, but he didn't seem to have noticed the stranger. "Did you see…?"

"Are your foster parents out there?" He peered through the glass, but I shook my head.

"No, there was this guy… never mind." Despite my words, tension settled across my shoulders that I couldn't quite shake. "Erm. How much did I tell you about my foster parents again?"

"You told me they were recently waterskiing in Australia to celebrate their retirement."

So I had. "I guess that gives a vivid enough picture."

A waterskiing retired couple formed quite the mental image, but I didn't know if their sudden liking for extreme sports would get past the aura of *otherness* that hovered almost imperceptibly over my father despite the glamour covering him from head to toe. The same aura doubtless covered me as well, but I'd lived with them for long enough that they might have been attuned to it.

Dad gave me a reassuring smile. "You were happy with your foster parents, and that's all that matters."

"You aren't wrong." Being in foster care could easily have been a much worse experience for a misfit like me. I cast a look around the café and saw a group of bedraggled shoppers eyeing our table hopefully, probably thinking we were about to leave. "Ah… we should probably order our drinks."

I'd forgotten that in a normal coffee shop, you had to go to the counter to order a drink rather than picking up a menu, tapping your order with your fingertip, and receiving your drinks without even needing to leave the table. Just one of the perks of the magical world I'd grown used to.

The moment I rose to my feet, an older couple walked into the cafe. Grey-haired and beaming, Mr and Mrs Wilkes descended on our table and draped me in hugs that unintentionally showered our table in rainwater.

"Blair!" Mrs Wilkes exclaimed. "It's so good to see you."

"Glad you got out of the rain," added Mr Wilkes. "Horrible, isn't it?"

"Yeah." I looked between them and Dad, who'd half risen to his feet. "Mum, Dad, this is… Dad."

"Call me Braden." He held out a hand to shake Mr Wilkes's hand then his wife's.

"You look so young!" Mum exclaimed.

Should have seen that one coming. Mum and Dad didn't see the glamour hiding his wings, but they did see that my dad's features did not resemble those of someone old enough to have a daughter in her midtwenties. He looked the same age as I did, in fact. Awkward.

"Genetics," I blurted. "I take after him, I think. Lucky me."

I wasn't kidding. While I wasn't immortal like a true fairy, I'd age slower than the average person and would always look younger than my actual age. I didn't like to think too hard about that, since I'd barely passed the point of being asked for an ID whenever I bought alcohol as it was, but I supposed it was better than being permanently stuck at the same age the way vampires were.

Time to change the subject. "We were about to order our drinks. Want me to get yours?"

"Oh—no, thank you, Blair," said Mrs Wilkes, pulling up a chair to join us. "We'll wait our turn."

Once we were all settled with our mugs of coffee or hot chocolate, my foster parents began questioning my dad on how we'd reconnected as adults. I'd seen it coming, so Dad and I had prepared our cover story thoroughly.

"How did Blair come to find you?" Mr Wilkes asked him.

"I once lived in this area," Dad replied. "When I was married to Blair's mother. Unfortunately, she died when Blair was only a year old. At the time, I was working a very demanding and dangerous job that made it impossible for me to take care of a child at the same time. I'm glad she was able to find a home with you, but if I have one regret, it's that I didn't stay in touch."

"Oh, I'm so sorry about your wife," Mrs Wilkes said. "That must have been so hard for you."

Dad gave a tight nod. "Yes… I miss her a lot. And I'm glad that Blair was able to track me down when she moved here."

We'd concocted a fake reunion story that left out the part about him being locked in jail when I'd first learned of his existence. Without the context—the least of which was that he'd been locked up for a crime he'd never committed—it'd only add unnecessary complications to an already elaborate cover story. Especially when it came to explaining how he'd earned his freedom. In the process of securing his release, my allies and I had had to outwit Inquisitor Hare—aka Rowe Clearwater, a fairy who'd masqueraded as the human head of the paranormal hunters—and I'd narrowly avoided jail myself. Since the

Inquisitor hadn't been seen since I'd thwarted him, there was no sense in opening old wounds and potentially setting up my foster parents for trouble, so we stuck to the cover story.

From the questions they fired at him, they thought my dad had a top-secret job as a superspy or something, which was kind of hilarious, given that he sometimes struggled to turn on light switches and other modern necessities. After all, he'd gone from living in the realm of the fairies to being on the run before his stint in jail, so he hadn't exactly had much time to learn his way around the technology of the human world.

Then again, given that my foster parents often needed my help with their smartphones, I figured they could use that particular struggle as a bonding exercise. In any case, we got through the questioning part of the visit without accidentally straying close to mentioning the magical world, and Dad was adept at playing along. When the rain had cleared and we'd finished our coffees, I suggested we have a look around the shops.

We hadn't taken two steps before a commotion arose from outside the shopping centre. I turned to the window and saw that a crowd had gathered around someone lying on the ground outside. With a quiver of unease, I recognised the prone stranger as the man I'd seen pushing through the crowd in a state of panic earlier. Right now, though, he wasn't moving at all.

"What's wrong with him?" Mrs Wilkes craned her neck to see through the window, but everyone else had had the same idea.

Amid the noise of the gathering crowd, I made out a few words.

"He just collapsed…"

"Not breathing…"

"I think he's dead."

The last whisper chilled my blood, and the sound of sirens caught my attention. While the people from inside pressed their faces to the window, my instinct drove me towards the door. Dad caught my eye and nodded.

"I think we should go," I told my foster parents. "Before it gets too crowded out there."

"Oh, what an awful thing," Mrs Wilkes commented. "I hope they can help him."

"Poor fellow," added Mr Wilkes.

We got to our feet and made our way to the exit. When we emerged near the crowd outside, I heard one loud voice saying, "They say he just dropped dead, but there's nothing medically wrong with him."

Weird. He didn't look that old, and he'd seemed perfectly fine not long beforehand, despite his notable urgency in the way he'd moved through the crowd. The notion that the man's death might have had a magical cause crossed my mind, but I'd have to wait until my dad and I were alone together to ask if he'd picked up on anything that I hadn't.

"You might want to leave now if you want to beat the traffic," I told my foster parents. "It's been great seeing you, though."

Mr Wilkes wrapped me in a hug. "We'll see you soon, all right, Blair?"

"Of course." I hugged Mrs Wilkes, and then Dad and I stood side by side for a moment to watch their departure.

Meanwhile, the crowd in front of the shopping centre

gradually dispersed as the unfortunate man was lifted into the ambulance.

"Do you think his death had a magical cause?" I asked in a low voice.

"Might have," Dad murmured back. "But it's unlikely. I didn't see anything odd."

"Nor me." Of the two of us, I was the one who had the ability to tell what type of paranormal someone was by looking at them, but when he'd been in the middle of the crowd, I hadn't been paying full attention. It was too late now, since my ability didn't work on the dead, only the living.

"So much for nothing going wrong," I whispered. "They'll think I'm a bad-luck magnet… which isn't really news to them, but still."

"I think the meeting otherwise went well," he said. "I'm proud of you."

"You're the one who gave the best performance." I gave him a faint smile, some of my apprehension easing. "Let's go back to Fairy Falls."

I did my best to put the strange man's death to the back of my mind as we left the town centre behind, though I had to wonder if I should pick a different meeting place next time. It might not make a difference, considering my uncanny ability to attract trouble had only intensified since my induction into the magical world. My foster parents were already acquainted with my penchant for ending up mired in chaos, but there was a limit.

Sometimes I wished I could let them in on the truth, but it wasn't worth the risk, and besides, the magical world was a major culture shock to the uninitiated. I'd barely managed to cope with the adjustment, despite being half witch, half fairy, and all weird.

Once we'd left Sloan behind, Dad and I snapped our fingers to remove our glamour as we began the flight across the countryside towards Fairy Falls, our wings more than making up for the lack of public transport in the area. The magical community where I'd lived for almost a year now was impossible to find on a map, and while the grass wasn't exactly greener on the other side, it did look more inviting to my eyes. Soon, rolling hills and wild forests surrounded us, and the glittering lake that marked the town's eastern edge drew closer with every beat of our wings.

As we reached the foot of the hill nearest to the town, I spotted three figures approaching the boundary of Fairy Falls. One was a woman who looked around my age with windswept dark-brown hair and pale skin. The second person was a teenager with a pair of bright-red goggles perched on her head. Odd, but not as much as their third companion—a ghost. Older than the girl but still likely in his teens, he drifted up and down the hillside and whistled what sounded like "The Imperial March" from the *Star Wars* movies. I tilted my head, trying to figure out if the other two were aware of their ghostly ally or not. Dad, of course, could see only the two humans, and he gave me a questioning look, asking how to proceed.

I snapped my fingers to hide my fairy wings before approaching their group. "Excuse me?"

All three strangers turned towards me, the ghost included. I'd already figured that they must be paranormals, because if they weren't, the town's magic would have turned them around and sent them back to the ordinary world. A closer look confirmed the teenager was a witch, but the other two were less clear. Especially the woman. Her gaze travelled over me as though performing a similar assessment.

"Hey there. Are you from this town?" the woman asked.

"Yes, I am," I said. "If you're not, what are you doing here?"

My tone sounded more accusing than I'd intended, but what kind of paranormal was she? The young girl was a witch, clearly enough, but while I detected a similar vibe from the woman, there was something else there too. Whatever it was, it gave my paranormal-sensing power pause. *She's not a fairy, is she?*

She lifted her head to meet my gaze. "We're here to stay in Fairy Falls for a few days, and we have a reservation. I'm Maura."

"A reservation?" I echoed. "Sorry. That should be fine then. I'm Blair."

"And I'm Carey," the girl with the goggles on her head said brightly. "Sorry, we just walked in here. There's not really a footpath, and the wards are strong."

"There should be someone on security duty. I'll check."

Nathan was head of the town's security team, in name at least, but the actual rota was Steve's responsibility, and I was willing to bet that the grumpy gargoyle had dragged Nathan's team off to fill out some pointless paperwork instead of actually doing their jobs. Since this side of town was the one part that didn't border on the territories of the werewolves and didn't have a lake in the way, the strangers' unnoticed arrival wasn't as suspicious as I'd initially thought.

"All right," said Maura. "We'll be staying at the... what's the name again, Carey?"

"Lakeside Inn," the girl answered promptly.

"Is there a reason you chose to come here on holiday?" I glanced at my dad, who seemed as puzzled as me. Fairy Falls wasn't on the usual tourist maps and didn't produce much interest even for most paranormals unless there was a particular event happening.

"We're here to look for ghosts," Carey told me. "I found an interesting news story about a ghost who haunts this lake, and since I run a ghost blog, I wanted to see if we can uncover anything."

"Ghosts?" If not for her sincere tone, I'd have wondered if she was having me on. Ghosts didn't show up that often, and I certainly hadn't heard of one being well-known enough to have reached an audience outside of the immediate community.

"Yep," Carey said. "I brought my camera and everything."

Hmm. She was more of an expert than I was, and the fact that she and Maura had brought a ghost of their own as a companion was proof enough that they knew what they were talking about. While about a third of witches and wizards could see ghosts, I hadn't known spirits ever travelled around with living people. Or that they accompanied them on ghost-hunting holidays, come to that.

"All right," I said. "The Lakeside Inn..."

"I don't know where it is," the girl piped up. "Can you show us?"

"I imagine it's by the lake," Maura said dryly. "Unless they decided to be contrary and stick it on a hill instead. Not everywhere is like Hawkwood Hollow, though."

"Is that where you came from?" I began to walk towards the lake, and so did my dad. He'd hidden his wings, but I had to wonder if the three of them had ever seen a fairy before. The average magical community didn't have many, and most of ours had moved here recently thanks to our efforts to put the town back on the map as a safe haven for fairies.

"Yep," Maura answered. "Whoever built our town decided to number the houses at complete random, so if you've got that sorted, it's an improvement."

"They've got the creepy signage right," said the ghostly teenager, indicating the crooked sign saying "Fairy Falls."

"So they have." Maura gave the sign an approving nod. "Did someone tilt that thing on purpose?"

"I haven't the faintest idea." I'd thought the sign had horror-movie vibes the first time I'd seen it, but that was before I'd known ghosts and other magical monsters were a genuine possibility.

Carey lowered her goggles over her eyes and fiddled with a dial on the side. "I've got to get a picture of that."

A clicking noise sounded. Was her camera somehow hidden inside those goggles?

"Ah—how many blog readers do you have, exactly?" I asked her.

Carey pushed up her goggles again. "I don't remember. A dozen, maybe? One of them's my mum."

Ah. I decided not to mention my relief, since I wasn't certain the other residents were prepared for an influx of tourists yet. Granted, the town was picturesque when it wasn't drenched in rain, with the glittering lake forming a backdrop. Maybe we did need to boost our tourism profile.

A reflection on the water signalled the approach of someone else walking down the path alongside the lake. *There he is.* Tall and broad-shouldered, dark-haired and handsome, Nathan was the first person I'd met in Fairy Falls and also the man who I usually saw when I woke up in the morning. A grin tugged at my mouth. I should have known he'd come to check up on the security situation despite Steve's best efforts.

"I'll see you later," I said to my dad. "And you," I added to the newcomers, who were still snapping pictures of the lake.

Hurrying up the path, I came to a halt in front of Nathan. Instead of his usual smile, he greeted me with an expression that he might wear if I'd tripped over the dead body of that poor guy at the cafe.

"Hey, Nathan… is something wrong?"

"That woman you were talking to," he said. "Did you know she was a Reaper?"

A what?

What in the world was a Reaper?

2

When I voiced my question aloud, Nathan gave me an odd look. "You don't know what a Reaper is?"

"Evidently not." Now I felt like a fool. "It's one of those basic *Magic for Dummies* questions that I should have learned the answer to when I was about four, isn't it?"

"No... not exactly," he said. "The town doesn't have a local Reaper, so it's not surprising that the question has never come up in the past."

Heat rushed to my face. "Well... I've heard of the Grim Reaper. Is that a thing?"

"Some of them are certainly grim," he said. "Their main job is to help the dead move on to the next world."

"That explains why they came here looking for ghosts, then."

His brows shot up. "Ghosts? Here?"

"Apparently." I glanced over my shoulder, but the group of newcomers remained fixated on the lake, no longer paying me any attention. "I guess that's why I couldn't quite get a handle on her paranormal type, since I've never seen a Reaper before. The teenager is definitely a witch, though. I'm not sure about the ghost."

"The *ghost?*"

"Right… you can't see him." Not all witches could see ghosts, either, but being able to see them was a long way from whatever a Reaper did. "There's a ghost with them. A travelling companion, I'm guessing."

"A travelling companion?" His gaze passed over the lake, confusion furrowing his forehead. "Reapers usually send ghosts packing. They don't invite them on holiday."

"You can ask her if you like, but I thought you might want to talk to me instead." I gave him a smile, and this time, he returned it.

"I would," he answered, kissing me lightly. "Unfortunately, Steve has other ideas. He wants me to double my security force by the end of the month."

"I thought he didn't like you being in charge of the team at all."

"That was before he realised it gave him a new way to exert control over me," Nathan said. "I might run the team, but he's the boss."

"Typical." I'd bet it gave Steve no shortage of joy to make Nathan's life difficult. "What does he want you to do? Go around knocking on people's doors to ask if any of them want to spend every waking moment answering to a cranky gargoyle?"

"The theory is that the more people I recruit, the fewer shifts will be assigned to each team," he said. "Unfortunately, I think Steve is mistaken on the actual population of the town, let alone the percentage whose life goal is to work for him."

"Numbers aren't his strong point," I agreed. "Anyway, good luck with that. I'll head home. Alissa's probably waiting to hear how the meeting went."

He pressed a hand to his forehead. "Right, how did it go? I never asked."

"It went… great." Until someone had dropped dead, that was, but Nathan had quite enough to worry about without my adding the news of a normal's unfortunately timed collapse on top of it. Besides, my dad had seemed certain that the man's death hadn't had a magical cause, so there was no sense in spreading panic. "See you tonight?"

"I hope so," he said. "Though when Steve finds out we have a Reaper in town, I bet he'll find it a great excuse to triple our patrols."

"Not if you don't tell him."

"You're asking me to lie to Steve?" His tone was light, but I didn't miss the way his gaze strayed to the lakeside where the strangers had been standing. "I'll be the one he'll blame if our visitors end up getting into trouble."

"They're on holiday, aren't they?" I pointed out. "Even if they are looking for ghosts, that's unlikely to cause any issues, is it?"

"You'd be surprised," he remarked. "Anyway, you're right… they're on holiday. I'll tell Steve that and see how he reacts."

"And hope he doesn't *overreact*," I added. After all, the town's chief of police was not known for his pleasant manner or calm temper, and the fact that he was largely viewed as a joke by the population at large did not help matters much.

Nathan kissed me goodbye. "See you soon, Blair."

"Best of luck." I waved him off, watching the lake's

shimmering surface for a few more moments before heading for the main part of town.

Fairy Falls was a haven of cobbled streets and greenery, with the sound of the waterfall audible in the background when the noise levels were low. My home, a picturesque large house cloaked in ivy, still looked like something out of a fairy tale to me. I'd lived there for a year now, thanks to the generosity of Madame Grey, the leader of Fairy Falls's main coven. Her granddaughter, Alissa, sat reading a textbook on the sofa as I entered the large house and unlocked the door to my flat. Her familiar, Roald, lay napping next to her, while my own cat was sleeping on the armchair.

"Hey, Alissa." I left my shoes and coat by the door and then approached the armchair. Sky stirred, stretching out his arms and legs so he occupied twice the space he had previously. I perched on the arm of the chair and gave him a stroke.

"Hey." Alissa glanced up from her textbook. "How'd it go?"

"Mostly great." I attempted to gently shunt Sky aside to make room on the seat, but I might as well have tried to move a boulder. "No incidents, aside from a guy who dropped dead outside..."

Alissa put down her textbook with a *thunk*. "Honestly, Blair. Only you could say 'it was fine except someone dropped dead' with a straight face."

"He wasn't magical," I clarified. "My dad said there was nothing strange about his death. Except us being there, but if I counted every stroke of bad luck in my life as magical, I'd have had to meet my foster parents in a padded cell."

Alissa picked up her textbook and placed it on the coffee table. "I'd say the guy who died was unluckier than you were, personally."

"You aren't wrong," I acknowledged. "He's not the weirdest person I've seen today. That honour goes to the people we ran into on the way back to town."

Alissa gave an eye roll. "By 'weird,' do you mean fairies?"

"No, tourists," I answered. "I didn't think we *got* tourists here, but they said they were on holiday."

"That's not a bad thing." Her expression relaxed. "Maybe we're getting some good press. What kind of tourists were they?"

"A witch, a Reaper, and a ghost." A pause. "I assume the ghost was a tourist too. I didn't ask."

Alissa paled. "Did you say a *Reaper?*"

"Does everyone know what a Reaper is except for me?" I managed to wedge myself into the gap between Sky and the side of the armchair, with difficulty. "Nathan seemed on edge when he told me, but they're definitely here on holiday. I think my lie-sensing power would have told me otherwise." *Wait. Does it work on Reapers?* I'd have to check when we next ran into one another. We would, I had no doubt.

"I didn't know Reapers took holidays," Alissa commented. "Anyway, it's not the soul-reaping tendencies that are the problem. It's the fact that they're *creepy.*"

"Creepy?" Maura had been a bit abrupt in her assumption that she could just stride into town, but I wouldn't have used the word "creepy" to describe the woman or her teenage companion. Even her ghostly friend had seemed ordinary enough, aside from him being, well, dead. "I didn't get that vibe. I also couldn't sense that she was a Reaper until Nathan told me, so I guess we've found another exception to my paranormal-sensing abilities."

"That doesn't surprise me." She gave a shudder. "I'm not sure Reapers are even human. Not that that's a bad thing, but they're a literal world apart from regular people. Goes with the territory, I guess."

"She had a teenage girl with her," I said. "A witch."

"Huh." A furrow appeared in her brow. "I didn't think Reapers spent much time with other paranormals either. They tend to keep to themselves."

"I wouldn't know." Curiosity reared its head. "Have you ever met one?"

Alissa gave Roald a stroke. "Only twice in my life, but both left quite the impression. The long black cloak and scythe tend to stick in the mind."

"She didn't have a scythe. Nor a long cloak either."

"No scythe?" Alissa's lips pursed. "Weird. I'd say she must be retired, but I'm fairly sure Reapers aren't *allowed* to retire. It's a job for life. Or afterlife, as it were."

"You mean they're immortal?" I'd assumed the fairies were unique in that respect, but perhaps I'd been mistaken.

"I think they are, but they don't like to share their secrets with outsiders," she replied. "I only know because my grandmother has occasionally needed to meet with them as part of her duties as the coven leader. They basically exist for their work, and that's it. If they're needed, they show up in town, reap souls, and disappear."

"Yeah, that doesn't sound like the woman I ran into," I said. "I wouldn't have known she was a Reaper if Nathan hadn't told me. Though it explains why she had a ghost following her around."

"She had a *ghost* with her?"

"Yes. Is that odd? I know ghosts are usually tied to one place."

"Exactly," she said. "And yes, that *is* odd, especially for a Reaper. Their job description demands that they send any soul they encounter into the afterlife."

"I think it's safe to assume they aren't typical, then," I decided. "Nathan is going to tell Steve as a precaution, but I'd rather their holiday isn't ruined by him sticking his nose in."

"Yeah, I wouldn't be a fan of that either," she said. "Still, I have questions."

"Ask her, not me." I tilted my head. "Tell you what, we can offer to show them around town. They're bound to have a lot of questions themselves, since they knew nearly nothing about Fairy Falls when I asked."

"Hmm." She still looked a little discomfited. "I can't say I wanted to spend the evening with a Reaper, but I'd like to know what they're doing in Fairy Falls."

"The girl, Carey, mentioned looking for ghosts. Shouldn't be too hard for a Reaper, right?"

"Looking for ghosts, huh?" She rose to her feet and stretched. "I could use some fresh air. Where are they staying?"

"The Lakeside Inn." I climbed off the armchair, and Sky gladly took my place. "We might want to give them the tour before it starts raining again."

"And before the shops close for the evening," she added over her shoulder, picking up her shoes from the rack near the door. "Reaper tourists, huh. Those two words work together about as well as a vegetarian shark."

I snorted. "When you meet Maura yourself, you'll see that she's perfectly normal."

"By your standards, Blair, that means she's bonkers."

I mimed throwing a cushion at her.

As it turned out, we didn't need to go to the lake to find the newcomers. After we left the house, we found the three tourists wandering around the high street, peering into the windows of each shop. Well, two of them were. The ghostly teenage boy drifted along in the background, humming a tune and occasionally pulling faces at a group of passers-by. From their lack of reaction, they couldn't see him, but Maura certainly could. After he made to approach a group of schoolkids, she gave him a stern look worthy of Madame Grey, and he drifted away, mouthing "Spoilsport."

Then she caught sight of me. "You again. We're just checking out the sights here before it gets dark."

"This is Alissa." I practically had to drag her forward, since she'd come to a complete halt when Maura had looked in our direction. "My flatmate and granddaughter of the leader of the Meadowsweet Coven. We thought you might appreciate someone to show you around."

"Hey," Maura said to Alissa. "I'm Maura, and this is Carey."

She didn't introduce their third companion, perhaps assuming we couldn't see him.

Alissa, though, wore an expression that suggested Maura might as well have been the ghost herself. "Have you introduced yourself to Madame Grey yet?" she asked.

"Who?" asked Maura.

"My grandmother," Alissa replied with none of her usual cheeriness.

Maura's expression remained blank.

She didn't know about the local covens? Had they done no research at all before coming here? If they'd solely been looking at ghosts, then maybe it wasn't a surprise that they hadn't, but I didn't entirely blame Alissa for being edgy.

"They're tourists, Alissa," I said. "They don't need to meet your grandmother unless they're here for witch-related reasons."

Alissa shifted her weight. "Not to be a killjoy, but I'm fairly sure my grandmother will find out pretty quickly if I let a Reaper come to town and didn't tell her."

Oh boy.

Maura went completely still. Her demeanour shifted from casual to tense, and with her steely expression, she wouldn't have looked odd with a scythe in her hands after all.

"Who told you that?" She directed the question at Alissa.

"My boyfriend—Nathan—saw me talking to you at the lake," I hastened to explain. "He said you were a Reaper, but since I've never met one before, I didn't know."

Alissa cleared her throat. "The last Reaper I met had a scythe and wore a hooded cloak that covered his face, so I'll have to take Blair's word for it, but I think it's probably for the best if I at least let my grandmother know you're here anyway."

I nudged her in the side, keeping a wary eye on Maura. "Why?"

Nathan had already planned to tell Steve, but we didn't want to scare away our first tourists in forever, did we?

"We don't want trouble," Carey blurted.

Maura lowered her hands, but her posture remained tense. "I really didn't want to have this conversation."

"I did," said their ghostly friend. "I told you that you wouldn't be able to get away with wandering around magical communities and *not* being recognised as a Reaper."

"Do you do this a lot, then?" I asked both Maura and Carey. "Travel around looking for ghosts? Is that normal in… what did you call it, Hawking Hollow?"

I'd never heard of the town, which wasn't that unusual given the gaps in my knowledge of the magical world. Just when I'd thought I was getting a grip on things, along came a Reaper, and I remembered how much I still had to learn.

"Hawkwood Hollow," Maura corrected. "We flew here to check out the local ghosts, not tell the entire town that I'm a Reaper. Or half Reaper, if you want to be specific."

"Half Reaper?" Alissa echoed. "So… oh, you're not an active Reaper?"

"I'm not, and I never have been," Maura told her. "That's why I don't make a habit of telling everyone I meet. One of the reasons."

"So you're half… witch?" That explained the confusion she'd caused in my paranormal-sensing power.

She inclined her head. "I'm not a standard witch either, but that leads to fewer questions. The only Reaper-related thing I'll be doing here is looking for ghosts."

"Which ghosts?" I indicated her incorporeal friend. "Not that one?"

"You can see me!" the ghost exclaimed.

"Is that odd?" I glanced at Alissa, whose attention remained on Maura instead of her ghostly companion. "I thought about a third of witches could see ghosts."

"Usually, yes," Maura responded. "Not where we come from, though. One of the reasons Mart wanted to come was to meet more people who he can actually have a conversation with."

"I can speak for myself." The ghostly teenager flew in front of Alissa and me and held out a hand to shake mine. "I'm Mart, Maura's brother. I'm the superior sibling, as you'll soon find out."

"Uh-huh." I bit back a grimace when his ghostly hand passed through mine with a shock of cold. "How did this come about? Why do you have a ghost travelling with you?"

"Long story," Maura replied. "Also, he's going to be absolutely insufferable now. Just so you know."

Mart pouted. "How cruel of you."

"Nice to meet you." Alissa dubiously accepted his outstretched hand and took a sharp step back when she got the same icy shock he'd given me. "I've never met a Reaper ghost, either."

"I'm unique." Mart twirled on the spot. "Right, Maura?"

The tension had notably eased, and I was all too happy to keep it that way. "We'll give you the tour. That okay, Alissa?"

To my relief, she gave a nod. "Sure."

Alissa and I led the way down the high street, showing the newcomers all the main shops they might need and giving the usual advice about not wandering into the werewolves' territory in the forest. If they were intending to go looking for ghosts, then they might find themselves out of bounds, and after the incident at the border, I wanted to be clear that not everyone would be as understanding as my dad and I had been. I decided against mentioning Steve unless absolutely necessary, but when we reached the lake again, I got a message from Nathan saying that Steve had ordered him to take out a security patrol and that he wouldn't be home until late. Typical.

"Nathan?" Alissa guessed, seeing my face when I checked my phone. "What's Steve done this time?"

"You're getting good at reading my mind. Is Samuel giving you lessons?"

She grinned. "Nah, you're just easy to read. Also, Steve makes demands of Nathan every other day. It's not hard to guess that he's the one bothering you."

"Fair enough," I acknowledged. "He's asked Nathan to lead an extra patrol tonight."

"Hope it stays dry, then." She cast a glance upward. "Looks like a storm's on the way."

Given the temperamental weather of the region in May, I wouldn't count on it staying clear for longer than an hour. "Want to get takeout or go to the Troll's Tavern?"

"Either." Alissa eyed our companions. "Do you guys want to come to the local pub?"

"That sounds good," Carey said.

"Sure," Maura agreed. "Lead the way."

I turned away from the lake, and we retraced our steps into the town, dodging the first raindrops as we entered the Troll's Tavern's cosy atmosphere. Nobody looked twice at us, which was one of the reasons I liked the pub so much. Since I often came here with Nathan, he did a fairly effective job of driving off the occasional person who wanted to stare at the fairy-witch, but I was mostly able to blend in. The majority of the stares had stopped in the last few weeks as the novelty wore off, and even Mart didn't attract much attention, despite his insistence on drifting around and making faces at the other patrons.

"Mart," Maura hissed at him. "Behave or I'll send you outside. If you scare the locals, then nobody will want to help us."

He sighed but obeyed, and we ordered our food by tapping on the menu from the table we'd picked out by the window. It showed up within minutes, appearing on the table before us. While we ate, I took the opportunity to find out more about our visitors. Carey did most of the talking, which made sense since the ghost blog seemed to be hers. I did wonder how a Reaper—or half Reaper—had ended up helping her out, but Maura remained tight-lipped on the subject.

"We're here to find a specific ghost," said Carey. "Rumour has it that this ghost is known as the Shadow on the Lake."

"Never heard of it." I glanced at Alissa, but her expression showed no signs of recognition either.

"Me neither," Alissa said. "Samuel might know."

"Who's he?" Carey's eyes brightened. "A ghost expert?"

"An everything expert," I answered. "He's a librarian."

Alissa's vampire boyfriend worked at the library at the town's only university and was definitely the person to go to if you had a specific question on an obscure magical subject.

"Oh, good." Carey smiled. "When can we see him? Tomorrow?"

I gave Alissa a nudge, and she relented. "I don't see why not," she said. "He's always in the library, even on weekends. Also, he's a vampire, in case that's of interest."

Carey practically bounced up and down in her seat. "I haven't met a vampire before. Not up close."

"You haven't?" From what I'd heard so far, Hawkwood Hollow sounded like a strange town even by paranormal standards, although they might think the same of Fairy Falls.

"Yeah, we get mostly shifters and witches in our town," Carey replied. "And ghosts, but that goes without saying."

"Here, I'm unique." Mart waved to some people passing the window. "I like it."

"Don't get used to it," Maura told him. "We're here for a reason. We're going to find another ghost and get some footage for Carey's blog if all goes well. If not, we'll at least get a holiday."

"You post videos on your blog, then?" I asked Carey. "Is your audience usually paranormals, or does it include normals as well?"

"Mostly paranormals… but I try to hide the actual locations," Carey added. "So it's not easy for people to find us."

"Good," said Alissa. "I can think of a few people who'd have sharp words to say about footage of the town being haunted showing up all over the internet."

We could do with some good publicity but not if it involved messing with Fairy Falls's already precarious reputation. I didn't think fairies cared much about ghosts one way or another, but some people had zero desire to be haunted, while some, like Maura and Carey, sought the challenge.

As for me? I'd met a couple of ghosts in my time here, and they weren't that out of the ordinary in the magical world. Reapers, though… I was starting to get the impression that they were even rarer than fairy-witches, and that was saying a lot.

At Alissa's suggestion, Maura and the others agreed to meet up at the campus the following day to speak to Samuel. If anyone knew about local ghost legends, it was our resident vampire librarian.

3

The following morning, Alissa and I got ready to meet the others at the university campus. I'd wondered if Sky would show an interest, but he hadn't budged from his spot on the armchair since the previous night. I nudged him gently with a hand. "Want to come, Sky?"

"Miaow," he grumbled, otherwise not stirring from his sleep.

"All right then."

It seemed that ghosts weren't interesting enough to rouse Sky from his nap, so Alissa and I set off alone. It wasn't raining, though it'd drizzled again the night before, and the evidence was left behind in puddles on the wet cobblestones. For that reason, I wore my Seven-Millimetre Boots so that my feet hovered slightly above the ground, but I opted against bringing out my wings to fly uphill towards campus. I still wore my glamour most of the time around town out of habit, and while the university had taken a firm stance against the hostile attitudes some of its students had shown against fairies, I didn't need to invite another series of questions from the newcomers. They'd come here to hunt for ghosts, not fairies.

As planned, Maura and Carey waited for us outside the gate leading to the university campus, which covered the far northwest side of the town. The forest bordered our right-hand side, while the fence ahead of us marked the town's northernmost border.

Mart poked his head out from behind a tree. "Boo."

Alissa started. "Did you not hear a word we said about not going into the forest?"

"Mart thinks the rules don't apply to him," Maura said. "Don't worry, Carey and I have more sense."

Hoping she was telling the truth, I asked, "Ready to go to the library?"

"This is the right place, isn't it?" Carey indicated the fence circling the university campus.

"Yep, this is it." I gestured at the gate. "You might want to stay close together so you don't get lost. This place can get a bit confusing."

That was putting it mildly. Fairy Falls's sole university campus consisted of a maze of brick buildings painted in bright shades and decorated with murals depicting dragons, unicorns, and other mythical creatures. Alissa and I led the way while Carey stared around, wide-eyed, nearly getting knocked over a couple of times when broomsticks and bird familiars flew a little too low.

Even on the weekend, the campus was one of the busiest areas in town. A few dedicated groups of students practised spells, while another group of dishevelled witches attempted to rescue a flying carpet from a high rooftop, probably where they'd crashed it during a drunken flight.

I knew the route to the library well enough not to require a map or to ask for directions, but each visit to the campus brought a new batch of surprises. Our group had to detour around a miniature swamp that hadn't been there during my last visit and tiptoe past some shifters sleeping off hangovers on the lawn—some in human form, some not. You'd think the rain would have woken them up, but apparently not.

The library itself brought another level of bewildered awe to the uninitiated. Towering shelves extended to the ceiling and formed a maze that was all but impossible to navigate without some input from the resident vampire. Fortunately, he appeared at the door within seconds of our entry, gliding into view with the graceful speed that only a vampire could achieve.

Tall and dark-skinned and dressed in a mauve waistcoat, Samuel flashed us a fanged smile. "What brings you here at this time on a Sunday morning?"

It was closer to noon than dawn, but vampires had peculiar views of the time and tended to be night creatures. Just one reason that working in a university campus library was a perfect profession for a vampire.

"We're here for research purposes," I answered. "Or these two are."

I indicated my companions. Carey goggled at him for a few seconds, and even Maura looked slightly alarmed, possibly at the sheer speed with which he'd appeared. Vampires had that effect on anyone who didn't regularly interact with them, though Maura recovered quickly.

"Hey," she said. "I'm Maura. This is Carey. We're from Hawkwood Hollow."

"How interesting," said Samuel. "What made you pick our fine town as your holiday destination? I assume there's a particular purpose for your visit to the library."

"We're looking for information on local ghost legends." Carey found her voice. "One in particular. Have you heard of the Shadow on the Lake?"

"Funny you should mention it," he replied. "I believe that particular legend was mentioned in a magazine article recently about unsolved mysteries."

"I think that might be where I saw it too." Carey's manner relaxed a little, though her gaze kept darting to his fangs. "Do you know anything else about the legend?"

"I will have a look," Samuel said.

The shelves rattled as he vanished in a blur. Carey startled again, while Maura blinked a couple of times. "I forgot how dramatic vampires can be."

"I prefer the term 'stylish.'" The vampire was back already, arriving as swiftly as he'd departed, and he now held a bundle of old newspapers and magazines in his hands. "This is everything I have on the subject."

Carey's mouth swung open. "Ah… thanks."

Maura took the papers from the vampire. "I didn't know there'd be so many sources on the subject."

"Those are all the articles I have pertaining to ghosts seen near the lake," he clarified. "Including this Shadow on the Lake you seek out. It should be easy enough to identify which articles reference the spirit you're looking for."

Maura eyed the articles. "So you don't know which are relevant?"

Carey nudged her. "It won't be any trouble to take a look at them ourselves. Thank you."

"The ghost always appears near the lake, then?" I asked before the vampire could get annoyed at Maura for poking holes in his generosity. "Like the pirate wizard guy?"

"Pirate wizard guy?" echoed Carey.

"I met this ghost last summer who haunted the lake and fancied himself a pirate," I explained. "I never heard him referred to as 'the Shadow on the Lake,' so it's probably not the same spirit you're searching for."

"I doubt it." Maura carried the papers to a nearby table, tailed by Mart and Carey.

Alissa watched them leave. "Did you have those articles already prepared for them? Are you sure you aren't a Seer and not a vampire?"

"They're hardly the first people to come here asking about local legends around the lake," Samuel remarked. "As for that particular spirit, though, I'm inclined to think they'll be disappointed in what they find."

Wondering why he thought that would be the case, I went to check up on our visitors, mostly giving Alissa and Samuel some privacy to talk to one another. My best friend's hidden reckless streak meant it wasn't entirely a surprise to me that she'd picked a vampire as her boyfriend, but the two were well suited, and Samuel was positively mellow as far as vamps went.

Maura and Carey were in the process of arranging the various articles and clippings atop a table, while Mart hid behind bookshelves and pulled faces at anyone who passed by.

"What do you know so far?" I asked them.

"The ghost is said to appear at a certain place on the edge of the lake," Maura replied. "She casts a shadow—hence the name, Shadow on the Lake. Also, she always appears at midnight, and she has a habit of dragging people into the water if they get too close."

"Yeah, that isn't the ghost I ran into," I said. "You say this one's definitely a female ghost?"

"A witch," Carey put in. "The legend also says she puts a curse on anyone who looks directly at her. Or anyone who sees her face. It's a bit vague."

I raised a brow. "And you're still going to look for her? Don't you think that might be a hint that she wants people to leave her be?"

"It's abject nonsense," Maura said. "Ghosts can't curse people. They can't even use wands."

Oh, right. Of course they can't. "Who was this ghost when she was still alive, then?"

"Precisely what I'd like to find out." Maura moved a handful of newspaper clippings around. "Ghosts usually appear shortly after their death, but there's sometimes a short delay, so we can use the dates of her appearance to narrow down the time frame in which she died."

"Didn't the original article you read mention the date she first appeared?" I asked.

"Not a specific one," Carey answered. "There have been sporadic reports of incidents by the lake for years. Tourists telling stories of disembodied figures throwing stones at them and grabbing their hands, that sort of thing. They blamed merpeople at first. There are merpeople in the lake, aren't there?"

"Yes, and sirens, among other things." I glanced over at Mart, who was doing a ridiculous dance above the shelves. "A prankster merman is more plausible than a ghost. Some of them get a kick out of messing with humans."

"Maybe, but the article said the ghost has definitely been sighted in the flesh… or spirit, rather," Carey went on. "Recently too."

"Who wrote the article you read?" I pulled out my phone, figuring it was worth running a search on the article in question. "Not a local, right?"

I hadn't heard anything myself, but I was hardly aware of everything that went on in the magical world. In fact, as I'd learned recently, there was a variety of paranormals that I'd never been introduced to yet.

With my phone in hand, I typed "The Shadow on the Lake" into the search bar of the Wizarding Web and waited to see what came up. An article in the aptly named *Ghostly Magazine* was the first result, but the second headline leapt out at me: "Writer for *Ghostly Magazine* dies in freak accident."

My throat went dry. "Uh… did you know the article's writer died?"

"Seriously?" Maura rose to her feet and leaned over my shoulder to look at my phone screen. "Does it say when?"

"Recently." I skimmed down the page, which detailed the fate of the unfortunate writer. "He died in a car crash on his way back from a trip to report on ghost legends in the northwest of England."

"So the ghost didn't kill him, then," Maura concluded.

"That's how the curse is rumoured to work." Carey looked up at us, her eyes as round as saucers. "The ghost doesn't *directly* do anything to them, but people who encounter her often meet unfortunate ends later on."

A shiver ran down my spine. "The guy who wrote the article didn't actually see the ghost, did he?"

"The article doesn't make it particularly clear, and there's no photographic evidence." Maura left the newspaper clippings on the table. "That's what we came here to get. Right, Carey?"

"I guess…" Carey hesitated. "The ghost only comes out at midnight, though."

"You find out that the last person to look for the ghost died, and your immediate reaction is to go looking for her yourself?" I asked Maura incredulously. "And to take a photograph, at that?"

"I'm ninety percent sure the guy who wrote that article didn't set eyes on the ghost and a hundred percent sure she wasn't the cause of his death even if he did," she responded. "Besides, if there *is* a curse, I'm probably immune. Reapers usually are."

That meant there was still a risk to her teenage sidekick, but Carey didn't seem to be perturbed by Maura's proclamation. She gathered the articles together into a neat pile while Samuel glided over to our table. "Are you going ghost hunting already?"

"I think we are," said Carey. "Is it okay if we leave the articles to come back to later?"

She seemed overly optimistic that there'd *be* a later, but I decided against voicing that observation aloud. I might know magic to be unquestionably real, but there was a difference between magic and outright superstition, and the curse definitely fell into the latter category. Ghosts could sometimes use magic without the need for a wand, but they couldn't doom someone to meet an untimely death. Of that, I was certain.

"Of course," said Samuel. "I wish you the best of luck. I assume you have a strategy for finding this spirit?"

"I have a lot of experience with stubborn spirits," added Maura. "It won't be a problem."

Samuel wore an intrigued expression when he watched them leave, but he didn't give any indication that he knew she was a Reaper. While he could have read the information from her thoughts, he didn't always like to invade people's privacy.

Maura led the way out of the library. Carey bounded after her in excitement, as if she were going to Disneyland and not ghost hunting.

I snagged Alissa's sleeve. "Do you think we should supervise?"

A frown furrowed her brow. "You know, when I planned my weekend, I didn't account for hunting ghosts with a Reaper."

"You don't have to come, but I'll keep an eye on them."

"As if I'm going to let you go alone." She nodded to Samuel. "See you later?"

I gave Alissa an abbreviated explanation of the so-called curse while we made our way across campus. Upon reaching the gate, I had to talk Maura out of taking a shortcut through the werewolves' part of the forest, though Maura understood once I explained the pack's tendency to get a little hairy—literally—over perceived incursions on their home turf.

"I know all about territorial werewolves," commented Maura. "Since I'm dating one of them."

"Really?" That was a strange pairing. A werewolf and a Reaper. No weirder than a fairy-witch and an ex-paranormal hunter, though, I supposed. "But you came here alone…"

"He's busy at work."

I could relate, since I hadn't heard from Nathan since the message he'd sent me the previous evening. No doubt Steve had him running around the lake, looking for nonexistent threats. As opposed to us, who might be about to walk headlong into a genuine curse. I might not entirely believe the rumours, but given my own penchant for attracting disaster, tempting fate did not strike me as a great idea.

Alissa was even more sceptical than me. "There's no such thing as a curse which acts on its own without someone to actually cast it," she said. "Only a witch or wizard can curse someone, and while it's possible for a curse to outlast someone's death, that's only possible if it was cast on an object. A ghost is definitely *not* an object."

"Fair enough." I walked at her side, behind Maura and her friends. "How do you explain the fate of the article's writer, though?"

"Unless he took a cursed object into the car with him, I highly doubt that's what caused his death," said Alissa. "It's more likely that he got careless or dozed off after staying awake all night hunting ghosts."

I gave her a sideways look, dropping my voice. "Not that I disagree, but you were more freaked out by the idea of running into a Reaper than a ghost who can put a curse on people."

"That's because one of those things exists, and I became significantly less freaked out when it turned out that she isn't carrying a scythe."

"That we know of." If a Reaper's job was to banish

ghosts, then even if there *was* some kind of curse at work, Maura ought to be able to get rid of it, right? It didn't mean we had to go along for the ride, but if disturbing the ghost caused it to take out its ire on the rest of us, I'd rather be forewarned.

We took the shortest route through the witches' part of the woods to the path running alongside the lake. Carey kept stopping to pull her bright-red goggles over her eyes and snap photos of our surroundings. They made her look like she was about to walk into a sci-fi convention rather than hunt ghosts, but I supposed the camera function was handy.

"Can you even see through those?" I asked her. "Why not just use your phone or bring a regular camera instead?"

"They're designed to make it easier for me to see ghosts." She pushed them onto her forehead again. "Kind of. I'm still working on the next upgrade."

"Wait, you can't see ghosts?" Her obsession with them made even less sense, but it explained why she'd teamed up with Maura.

"No." She adjusted the goggles. "My regular vision is slightly impaired when I wear them, but I haven't figured out a way around that yet."

"You won't find many ghosts if you fall into the lake," Alissa remarked. "Be careful where you tread."

"I thought the ghost could pull people into the water anyway," I pointed out. "I'm inclined to blame that one on the merpeople, to be honest. I've definitely met some who'd find that amusing."

Cursing people to death, though? Not so much.

"That's amateur," Mart contributed. "Throwing stones

and dragging people around is a tame party trick. I can do much more than that."

He drifted over the lake and descended into the water, splashing all of us.

"Mart, cut that out," Maura told him. "The ghost won't show up if you keep fooling around."

Carey shielded her goggles from Mart's splashing. "The ghost is meant to appear on the other side of the lake. Is there an easy way across?"

"Not unless you want to swim," I replied. "Otherwise, you'll have to walk around the edge. The good news is that if you go south, you won't trespass on shifter territory."

"The bad news is that we might have to get out our broomsticks again," Maura commented. "Unless I try to draw the ghost's attention from here."

"Do you have the props for a ghost summoning?" I asked.

"I don't need them," said Maura. "If I check the after-world, then I can find out if there are any spirits hanging around."

I couldn't say I was a fan of that idea. "I thought you weren't a practising Reaper." I glanced at Alissa, whose expression suggested she wanted to make the same comment. "Or a trained one."

"Oh, I'm trained," replied Maura. "I just quit my apprenticeship before I fully qualified. Hence the lack of a scythe. Otherwise, I can still do most things that full Reapers can."

"And the Reaper Council just... lets you?" Alissa asked dubiously. "I thought they had strict rules. Really strict."

"Yes, they do." Maura's tone implied she didn't want to

discuss the subject. "But they're not involved in my life. I quit, and I'm pretty much as dead to them as the average ghost."

Alissa's raised brows showed me she had no more idea than I did of what we were about to witness. It was lucky there weren't any other potential bystanders in the area, though the sky was overcast and the grass too damp to sit on. Hardly the weather for a picnic by the lake.

"All right," Maura said. "Nobody panic."

As we watched, a patch of shadow spread outward from Maura's outstretched hands. Alissa stiffened beside me, her mouth hanging open, while Mart maintained a steady distance from his spot above the lake. Even Carey left her goggles off while Maura addressed the darkness in front of her. "Is anyone there?"

Silence responded, and I couldn't say I wasn't relieved that nothing had answered from within that creepy patch of darkness. All my instincts told me to get as far away as possible. The blackness could only be the afterworld, and it was definitely not a place the living wanted to be anywhere near.

I wasn't the only one who jumped violently when a figure popped up within the blackness, forming the outline of a young woman with long, curly hair. Carey hid her reaction by gripping her goggles, while Alissa grabbed my arm and then released it just as quickly, her expression sheepish. The ghost looked hardly out of her teens.

"Hey," Maura said to the ghostly woman. "Sorry to disturb you."

"No, you aren't." The ghost scowled at her. "Who are you, and what do you want with me?"

Maura stared for a moment as though taken aback.

"You're haunting the lake. Who are you? What's your name?"

"Mattie Lyons," answered the woman. "Why are you here?"

"To help you if you need it."

"I don't need your help," the ghost spat at her. "I need you to go away. All of you. Go far away and never come back."

"But I thought—" Maura broke off when the ghost turned on the spot and flew straight into the lake. A surge of water splashed all of us, and when I looked up, the ghost was gone.

I pushed a handful of wet hair out of my face, while Maura's wide eyes met mine. "Well… that was a bit more dramatic than I expected."

"You don't say?" Mart came drifting back from the lake, his expression peevish. "Someone's cranky about being disturbed. Rude of her if you ask me."

"Usually, ghosts are happy to accept my help," Maura said. "Or at least hear me out."

"Is she definitely gone?" Alissa looked uncertainly at the lake. "I thought she only appeared at midnight."

"Evidently, you woke her up," I told Maura.

"Guess she's never met a Reaper before," said Maura. "They tend to open up to us more than they do to regular people. I bet I can find her again if we stay."

"And get ourselves cursed?" I arched a brow. "Alissa, do you recognise the name Mattie Lyons? I assume she's a witch, or she used to be."

Alissa shook her head. "No. My grandmother might, but if we tell her, it'll invite all kinds of other questions."

Such as why a Reaper was in town, for instance.

Madame Grey had quite enough to deal with already. A stubborn ghost was nowhere near as important as wrangling the bickering members of the coven's council and preparing the entirely-too-young Head Witch to attend various meetings with the regional witch councils.

"I bet we can find out how she died," said Carey. "Ghosts don't just show up out of nowhere."

"No, they usually require someone to be dead first," Mart replied.

Maura rolled her eyes at her brother. "I'm assuming she died near the lake, since ghosts usually appear close to the place where they died or somewhere important to them. If I was a real Reaper, I'd wait for her to come back and then banish her."

"Have you ever acted like a real Reaper?" I enquired.

"No," Mart answered. "Never. Even when we were apprentices, she was allergic to all the rules. Sometimes she even made new ones up in order to break them."

"That's enough, Mart." There was no heat in her voice, however. "I'm not banishing her until we get some answers."

Carey gave Maura a worried look. "Good. Don't you want to know who she is and how she ended up haunting the lake?"

"Yes, and we're more likely to learn that from her than from anyone else." Maura faced the lake and addressed the world at large. "I can wait here all day."

Would the ghost come back if we waited long enough? She might, but if she refused to talk, we might not solve the question of who she was and how she'd died.

Not to mention where the rumours about curses had come from.

4

I went to work the following day with thoughts of our mysterious local spirit lurking in the back of my mind. While Maura and her friends had been content to wait around all day for Mattie's ghost to return, Alissa and I had gone home after the first hour, when it'd started raining again. As far as I knew, the ghost had neglected to show her face after her first appearance, but Maura didn't strike me as the type to give up easily, and Carey would stay as long as necessary to get some decent footage for her blog.

So far, all we'd got was a name. And no curses, but that went without saying.

A search on Mattie Lyons's name had yielded no results when I'd looked her up on the Wizarding Web, but that didn't necessarily mean she wasn't the ghost Maura and the others were searching for. Most witches didn't do anything important enough to end up in the history books, especially if they'd lived recently like Mattie presumably had. To get the list of past coven members, they'd have needed to go to Madame Grey, and considering Maura's reaction to being found out as a Reaper, she likely didn't want to draw attention from the authorities.

At least it didn't sound like Steve had gone after her yet despite his insistence on ordering Nathan to spend half the night patrolling by the town's southern border, as if he was worried another Reaper would come sailing across the lake if he turned his back. I could just imagine how the grumpy gargoyle would react to claims of a cursed ghost haunting the shores, so our best bet was to keep Steve at arm's length until Maura and her friends left town.

I reached the office of Eldritch & Co, and Callie, the blond werewolf receptionist, smiled in greeting as I walked in. On the left, a short corridor led to the office I shared with my three other co-workers. Rob, our newest co-worker and Callie's cousin, gave me a cheery wave when I sat down at my desk. He'd left mugs of coffee on all our desks—courtesy of the coffee machine made by Lizzie, our resident technological expert—and I took a grateful sip from mine while I loaded up my computer.

At my side, a curtain of dark hair separated me from Bethan, the daughter of the boss, who worked at three times the pace of the average person and made the rest of us look as if we were working in slow motion. It didn't help that I required caffeine to function, while Rob's cheery phone manner persisted even at the earliest hour and with the most stubborn client. He'd definitely taken some of the stress off the rest of us since he'd started working here. On the other side of the room, Lizzie was fixing some kind of issue with the printer, which was emitting hissing noises as if a serpent was trapped in there. Given that it was a magical printer, that wasn't entirely out of the realm of possibility. Working in paranormal recruitment was never dull, that was for sure.

After checking my emails, I turned to my list of tasks for the day, expecting another week of helping the various fairies who'd recently moved to Fairy Falls find employment. I'd also made a small project of seeking out fairies who'd grown up with human families like I had, but that was a slower process and one that our small office couldn't handle alone.

The topmost name on today's list of clients leapt out at me. "Looks like Samuel was serious about finding a fairy to help him out in the library after all."

"Who?" asked Bethan without looking up from her own teetering stack of paperwork. "Oh—the vampire librarian."

"Alissa's boyfriend." He'd specifically asked for a fairy, but it'd taken a few weeks for him to put in the application. "I have no shortage of fairies looking for work, so I'll see which have the relevant experience."

The number of places willing to hire fairies was lower than I'd have liked, though a lot of that was due to some fairies having the same issues with navigating the modern world as my dad did. The ones who'd grown up in the human world didn't have the same difficulties—like Buck, who was engaged to Nathan's sister Erin, for instance. But for some, long-held prejudices against fairies won out, and there was little I could do to mitigate it other than seeking out the employers who were more open-minded. I was glad Samuel had stuck to his word about picking a fairy as his assistant librarian. Wings would definitely be an asset when navigating that library.

I read over the profiles of the fairies who might be suited for the role before sending some emails inviting them to the office for interviews later. Once I was done with that, I found my thoughts wandering over to the mysterious ghost again. Or specifically, the so-called curse. During a lull in the others' phone calls and chatter, I decided to ask the office at large.

Addressing everyone in the room, I asked, "Have any of you heard of a witch called Mattie Lyons?"

"No," said Bethan. "Should we have?"

"I guess not." Come to think of it, my office computer had a more robust search engine than my phone did, and if Mattie had ever worked with Dritch & Co at any point, she'd show up in our database. "Never mind."

Since I had a little time before the interviewees showed up, I ran a search on her name and came up with a photograph of a sullen-looking witch of maybe eighteen. Her file didn't say much, only that she'd dropped out of the witch academy and had had a few interviews for jobs which had ultimately been unsuccessful.

I jumped when a voice spoke from behind me. "What are you doing, Blair?"

Swivelling around, I found my boss studying my computer screen. Veronica Eldritch looked almost the same as her daughter except her hair was white instead of black. Tall and lean, she moved faster than the average person and was as good at sneaking up on me as a ghost.

"Ah." I scrambled for an excuse. "I'm waiting for people to show up to interview..."

"It'll be hard to interview someone who's dead."

I blinked. "You know who she is?"

"Mattie Lyons?" She studied her image on my

computer screen. "Yes, I remember when she disappeared."

"Disappeared?" I knew the others were listening in curiously, but if Veronica remembered the ghost when she'd still been alive, it'd save us the bother of asking Madame Grey.

"Yes, a few years ago." Her expression turned thoughtful. "She was only eighteen or so at the time. I don't think they ever found her."

"But you know she's dead?" If she was a ghost, then that was a given, but I still wondered how she'd ended up haunting a lake of all places.

"That was what the police eventually concluded, I believe," said Veronica. "Don't you have interviews to prepare for, Blair?"

"Sorry, I got distracted." It didn't sound as if Mattie had an obvious connection to the Shadow on the Lake and its unsavoury reputation, but I knew better than to push my luck by asking the boss questions that had nothing to do with work. Maura would not be thrilled if she found out my entire office had found out the name of the ghost, but then again, I wouldn't have known Veronica had ever heard of her if I hadn't been caught.

Despite it all, I had even more questions than I had before, and it was clear that a simple online search wouldn't give me the answers. I'd need to dig deeper… and talk to Maura and the others again to see if they'd been able to get back in touch with the ghost.

———

After I left work at the end of the day, I had a magic lesson to go to before I'd be free to return to hunting ghosts. From the office, I made my way to the large house that served as the main base for the town's leading witch coven. Ivy curtained the redbrick walls, and the bright flowers in the front garden were in full bloom despite the lingering clouds in the sky. The heavy oak doors led into a wide entrance hall. I walked through the open doors into the classroom where I took my lessons in magic.

Rebecca smiled at me as I entered the classroom. The newest regional Head Witch, who'd just celebrated her twelfth birthday the previous week, was my only classmate, and the fact that she and I were both preparing for the same stage of magical assessments pretty much summed up how late in life I'd joined the magical world. Rebecca herself was a latecomer, too, not because she hadn't grown up in the magical world but because her scheming and controlling mother had kept her away from her fellow witches due to her abilities not exactly being the norm. I was pretty sure Rita had put us in lessons together as an incentive for me to try harder at mastering new spells, but Rebecca beat me nine times out of ten anyway.

Today was no exception. Rita had us practising hexes for the first time by using each other as target practise, and poor Rebecca was more at risk than I was. My ability to get the hang of spells was variable, partly because I was generally right-handed but had to use my wand in my left hand due to my fairy magic occupying the right hand—and partly because I'd always been clumsy and prone to a lack of coordination. Even discovering I was half fairy hadn't entirely fixed that issue, and the same routine plagued me whenever I had to learn a new spell.

"Focus, Blair." Rita's arms jangled with the various bracelets and bangles she wore as she gestured with her wand. "Hexes require focus, poise, and exact aim."

Easier said than done. Since hexes were the sort of magic that could go dramatically wrong if misapplied, I put in my best effort to keep my attention in the right place, but my first attempt at a croaking hex made Rebecca start emitting a noise that sounded more like a chicken than a frog.

"Close enough, Blair," said Rita. "All right, undo the hex."

Ah. I'd completely forgotten the wand movement to undo a hex. *It's a sweeping movement, right?* Hoping I was right, I swept my wand to the right and somehow made Rebecca spin like a spinning top, making chicken noises as she did so. Panicking, I cast a stopping charm, and she crashed headlong into the nearest desk, falling onto her rear.

"I'm sorry!" I yelped.

Rita undid the hex with a wave of her wand. "Really, Blair. Are you all right, Rebecca?"

"I'll be fine." She winced a little when she stood up, bringing a twinge of guilt. Her familiar, Toast, napped under her chair, oblivious to the mayhem around him. Sky rarely showed up to my magic lessons unless they required a familiar, and to be honest, I didn't mind there being one fewer witness to my frequent screwups.

"Your turn," Rita said to Rebecca. "Feel free to leave the croaking charm on for a bit to teach her a lesson."

"You're welcome to turn me *into* a frog as payback," I added lightly.

Instead of that, Rebecca cast the spell perfectly on the first attempt with no chicken noises to be heard. I opened my mouth and croaked loudly enough that the entire building could probably hear me. Heat rushed to my face, though I couldn't say I hadn't deserved it.

"A little overenthusiastic but good." Rita beamed at Rebecca. "Excellent work. I can see your practise is paying off."

My shame intensified. I didn't have too much free time to practise between my full-time job and magic lessons, but the truth of the matter was that I'd been too distracted by Maura's ghost hunt over the weekend to remember to do some preparation.

"Try again, Blair."

It took me six attempts to get the hex right, and even then only sporadically. If mastering a simple hex gave me this much trouble, then it was probably for the best that we wouldn't be moving onto curses for a very long time. Now did not strike me as the right moment to start asking questions about ghosts, but curiosity won out. When the lesson was over, I stayed back to talk to Rita alone.

"Blair," she said. "Did you want to ask me how to improve your wandwork? Because I can certainly offer pointers, but I think the problem today is your lack of attention."

She wasn't wrong there. "No, it's not about the lesson. I'll be sure to do some practise later."

"What is it then?"

"I wondered..." I hesitated. "There's a witch I heard

about who disappeared a few years ago. Have you ever heard of someone called Mattie Lyons?"

She frowned. "Where'd you hear of her?"

"Her name came up in connection with some local ghost stories," I said vaguely. "Also, my boss said she disappeared when she was only eighteen or so. I wondered if the case was ever resolved."

"I do remember the name," she said, "but she wasn't a member of our coven, so I can't say I know any more details. I assume the matter of her disappearance was dealt with by the police."

Hmm. That didn't mean Madame Grey wouldn't know anything more than Rita did, since she was familiar with all the local covens and not just her own, but the police would be more likely to hold the records of her disappearance.

"Thanks for letting me know," I said. "Erm… have you ever heard of the legend of the Shadow on the Lake?"

"Is that story still going around?"

"Still?" I echoed. "Erm, I read about it in a magazine this week, but it didn't say when the rumours started."

"There have always been rumours and superstitions concerning the lake," she said. "It's almost always the result of merpeople playing pranks on people or hapless normals seeing glimpses of the magical world and passing them off as hauntings. Don't trouble your mind about it, Blair."

I wasn't entirely convinced, but if anyone in the coven knew who Mattie Lyons was, Madame Grey was the person to ask. All the same, while the ghost case was peculiar, it wasn't more important than everything else the coven leader had to deal with. Unless a new development came along, I was better off leaving her alone.

I left the building and came to an immediate halt when I saw Maura and Carey coming the other way. Mart drifted along behind them, humming to himself.

"Are you here to talk to Madame Grey?" I asked them.

"We just wanted a look around," said Carey. "Is the coven leader in there?"

"Usually, she's in her office, but questioning Madame Grey about ghosts when she's busy working is not the best way to avoid attention from the authorities."

"Fair enough," said Maura. "I don't have the best track record with coven leaders anyway."

Mart cleared his throat. "That's an understatement. You chased the last one you met out of town."

"She did *what?*" I said, mildly alarmed.

"I assume this one isn't responsible for covering up murders, so it's fine," Maura said. "Okay, we'll go back to the library instead."

"Hang on one second." I wasn't about to let *that* go unquestioned, so I sped up to keep pace with her. "You chased your coven leader out of town for covering up murders? Do I have that right?"

"More or less," replied Maura. "Also, she wasn't my coven leader. I've never been a member of a coven."

I can't imagine why. "What were you doing near our coven's headquarters, then? Hoping to sneak a look at the records of current and past coven members?"

"How'd you know?" asked Carey.

"Because it's what I would do," I said. "Mattie Lyons wasn't part of the Meadowsweet Coven, though. I asked my boss, who would know."

I told them the little information I'd managed to glean from talking to Rita and Veronica. While Mattie's disappearance must have drawn attention at the time, I could only assume her death had remained undiscovered.

"Maybe she came back from the dead out of annoyance that her disappearance had been forgotten about," remarked Maura.

"Or to tell her family," Carey suggested. "Ghosts are often looking for closure, right?"

"If it's true, would her family take our word for it without seeing the ghost for themselves?" I asked. "I don't actually have the details on her family, mind. Have you talked to the ghost since yesterday?"

"No," Maura said. "I think she's avoiding me."

Weird. You'd think someone whose death had been unknown for years would have wanted for her family to know her fate.

"That's why we thought we'd go to the police," Carey put in. "They'd have the information on the case, wouldn't they?"

"If her disappearance was reported, the police will have the records," I acknowledged. "Though I can't say Steve will be willing to share them with you."

"Who's Steve?" asked Maura.

"Our gargoyle police chief," I said. "If you want to talk to *him*, then you're in for a real treat."

Despite my clarification of exactly why it was a bad idea, Maura and Carey decided to come and talk to the police right away, and nothing I said convinced them otherwise. After another failed attempt to find our elusive ghost, they'd spent most of the day in the library, separating the relevant newspaper articles on lakeside hauntings from the irrelevant ones, so they wanted to see some action.

"Most of the articles were referencing other ghosts, not ours," Maura told me. "Granted, we don't entirely know how Mattie Lyons came to be known as the Shadow on the Lake in the first place. I'm hoping learning the circumstances of her death will shed some light on that."

"It might," I acknowledged, "but you did hear me just tell you that Steve won't share police records with tourists, didn't you?"

"If she's not part of your coven, we have to get the

information from somewhere." Maura strode on, unde-terred. "How many covens are there?"

"I haven't a clue," I responded. "I was introduced to town via the Meadowsweet Coven, so that's the one I'm most familiar with. It's also the largest."

Aside from that, there was also my mother's former coven, the Wildflower Coven, but they no longer had any surviving members.

"So you didn't grow up here?" asked Maura.

"No." I didn't have the time to give them my entire life story, and mentioning being half fairy would only compli-cate matters anyway, but perhaps giving some context might help them see why Steve wasn't my biggest fan. "I grew up in the normal world. It's kind of a long story, but I had a run-in with the police in my first week here, and Steve has hated me ever since."

"Our town only has a single coven," Carey piped up. "Either you're with them or against them."

"I gather you're against them, considering you drove their leader out of town."

Mart laughed in the background.

Maura shot him a scowl. "I was trying to get her arrested instead, but she escaped and went into hiding. As soon as she shows her face in Hawkwood Hollow, there's a cell waiting for her. Drew—the guy I'm dating—is the head of the local police force, so he's as keen as I am to put her away."

That explained why she was confident that the police would willingly hand over the files. She was in for a rude awakening, since I was pretty sure Steve wouldn't hand any police records over to *his* girlfriend without good reason, let alone a group of strangers and his least favourite person in town. And for a guy who hated nearly everyone, that was saying something.

"I can guarantee that this won't go as smoothly for you," I warned as we rounded the corner onto the street where the police station was located. "Every single member of our local police department is a gargoyle shifter. Imagine a werewolf pack with its posturing turned up to a thousand and you'll get the picture."

"I've never met a gargoyle shifter before," Carey ventured.

"I have, but I can't imagine the average pack running an effective police department." Maura looked more intrigued than wary, though, and I had to wonder who'd win out of her and Steve in a battle of wills.

The wise decision was to drop them off at the doors and run for safety, but I abandoned that idea when I spotted Nathan in the lobby of the police station through the glass doors. Our gazes connected before I could come up with a decent explanation, and a brief spike of panic hit me when his gaze fell on Maura before common sense caught up. With Nathan here, I'd have at least one person to back me up if Steve started on his usual routine of obstruction and insults. Assuming Nathan himself didn't want Maura to stay out of the police's business, which was a distinct possibility.

The automatic doors slid open, and Nathan walked out. "Blair, what are you doing here?" *With them?* I imagined was what he really meant to say.

"Ah… hey, Nathan," I said. "We found the name of a ghost who's haunting the lake, and it sounds like her disappearance was never solved, so we wondered if the police had the official records. I did warn them."

His gaze slid to Maura and the others. "I'm sure the records are here, but we haven't the time to dig out an old case."

"What if nobody knew she was dead?" I felt compelled to speak up for the ghost despite her reluctance to communicate with anyone. "When we saw the ghost yesterday, she told us her name. I checked with Rita and my boss, and it sounds like she disappeared without a trace when she was only eighteen. I'm not sure if the case was ever solved, but if it isn't on record that she's dead, then I feel like it's something her family would appreciate knowing, at least."

"You aren't wrong, but whether Steve will see it that way is another matter entirely."

"He doesn't have to do anything himself." I didn't see Steve himself in the office, but that didn't mean he wasn't lurking around somewhere. "We just need a look at the file, nothing more."

It might not be worth risking the wrath of the gargoyle police chief, but Maura had no reservations. Without waiting to hear Nathan's reply, she sidestepped me and walked into the police station, striding right up to the reception desk.

Clare, who worked at the desk, lifted her blond head and asked in a bored voice, "Are you here to report a crime?"

"Possibly," Maura answered. "We ran into a local ghost who told us she died in odd circumstances, and I'd like to see the police's records of her death."

"That isn't going to happen," Clare said flatly. "Who even are you?"

"Maura Clarke," she replied. "This is Carey. We're professional ghost hunters."

Her brother pulled a face when she refrained from introducing him, but I assumed none of the shifters could see his ghost drifting through the lobby. Clare was usually more helpful than most of the other gargoyles, but that wasn't saying much.

A booming voice rang through the lobby. "So you're the Reaper."

My heart sank. None other than Steve himself shoved his way to the front of the police station, his tall frame dwarfing the desk. For some reason, the office itself was built to a regular human scale with the result that the gargoyles looked even larger than they actually were by comparison, especially their boss, who towered over all of us in his human form, let alone his gargoyle one.

Carey's mouth fell open, and she shuffled back a few steps, but Maura barely blinked. "That's me. I take it you're Steve?"

All my instincts screamed at me to get out, but Steve had already spotted me standing behind the newcomers. "Yes, I am. What do you want?"

Maura lifted her chin to look him in the eyes. "We're looking for information on a particular young witch whose ghost we found haunting the lake. I believe her death was unsolved."

"Not interested."

Carey flinched, but Maura met his eyes without fear. Someone who dealt with ghosts as frequently as she did was bound to find a gargoyle shifter less than impressive, but not being local didn't mean he couldn't lock her in a cell if he so desired.

I hastened to step in before things got too out of hand. "We'd just like to know if her death is on record, that's all. Nobody has ever spoken to her ghost before, and when I asked around, it sounds like she just disappeared without a single trace."

"How did I guess you'd managed to get yourself involved, Blair Wilkes?" he grumbled. "Whenever there's trouble, I can guarantee you'll manage to get mired in it."

A little unfair, even if he did have a point. "Surely it won't take long to check if the girl's family knows she's dead?"

"Why don't you go and bother Madame Grey instead of me?"

"Because the girl in question wasn't a member of her coven," I replied. "Her name's Mattie Lyons, and she died a few years ago—"

Steve cut me off by growling under his breath. "Whoever it is, I have better things to do than to riffle through our old records to suit your every whim."

If he was wandering around the office baring his teeth at people, then he clearly *didn't* have anything better to occupy his time with, but it was not a wise idea to point that out.

Maura, however, either didn't pick up on the tension in the air or simply didn't care. "It won't take you long to check the records. You could have searched for her name in the time it took to have this conversation."

"This is none of your business," he retaliated.

"It's my job to help lost souls move to the afterlife." Maura's manner changed subtly, and there was a new edge to her words that drew a chill to my arms. "Would you close your doors to the Grim Reaper himself?"

I looked at Maura in horror. Had she seriously just threatened Steve? He might not have had any direct experience with Reapers—or maybe he had; I didn't know—but that didn't mean he didn't know a threat when he heard one. The air thickened with tension, and I wondered if he might actually shift into his gargoyle form.

Instead, he loomed over Maura, his face inches from hers. "Get out."

Carey bolted. Mart was long gone, though nobody in the office had seen his ghostly presence. Maura met his gaze for a long, tense moment before shrugging and turning away. Relief swamped me when she left through the automatic doors, and I was all too happy to follow her out.

"Not so fast, Blair Wilkes," Steve boomed at me. "I know you brought these troublemakers here for the purposes of wasting my time. Didn't you?"

"Steve, that's enough," said Nathan firmly. "She was trying to help them, nothing more."

"Exactly." For a brief moment, I debated mentioning the curse and seeing how Steve reacted to *that*, but we'd all seen the ghost, and none of us had dropped dead yet. Besides, Steve would probably throw a party if I died as the result of an unfortunate ghost curse.

Outside, I found Maura comforting a shaking Carey. "He's all bluster, don't worry. I know his sort."

"He can still have you arrested," I warned her. "You're not doing the ghost any favours by losing your temper with the law enforcement, you know."

"Is he that unhelpful when an actual dead body shows

up?" Maura asked. "Or is his cavalier attitude reserved for unresolved cases?"

"Depends on whether or not he's personally inconvenienced," I replied. "He's in charge, unfortunately, so if he says no, that's it."

"Hmm." Maura cast a glare in the direction of the police station. "We'll see about that."

She walked away with Carey hurrying along behind her, leaving Nathan and I alone together.

"Your friend has a death wish," Nathan remarked. "I know that's probably a contradiction for a Reaper, since they're functionally immortal, but still."

"Not her." I dropped my voice in case she was listening in. "She's not a practising Reaper, or so she told me. She's half witch, half Reaper."

"Oh." A furrow appeared in his brow. "You don't have to help her, Blair. She seems the troublesome sort."

"Steve says the same about me," I reminded him. "Besides, it's the ghost I wanted to help. Maura… she's going to do her own thing whether anyone tells her otherwise or not."

My habit of sticking my foot in my mouth didn't extend to outright threatening the chief of police the way Maura had. Did the ghost's fate really mean that much to her, or was she just incapable of letting something go?

"I'd leave her to it," Nathan said. "Want to go to the Troll's Tavern?"

"Sounds perfect." I fell into step with him, glad to finally have time for an actual date. "I take it Steve doesn't have you patrolling tonight?"

"Not as of yet," he replied. "Steve didn't ask me to

come back in, so I can thank you for rescuing me from the aftermath."

"I think Maura put Steve in a bad enough mood to be a nightmare for the rest of the week, so I apologise for that," I said. "In fairness, I didn't think he'd be *that* stubborn. You'd think he'd jump at the chance to have an old file permanently closed."

"Steve doesn't care much for revisiting old cases," he said. "Besides, he can't see ghosts, so there's no chance of him taking this one seriously unless she starts haunting him directly."

"Don't give Maura ideas." Her brother was capable of doing exactly that, but as amusing as it was to imagine, the fallout would land on Nathan and the rest of us, not Maura herself. However this ghost situation turned out, she and Carey would be gone by the end of the week.

When we entered the Troll's Tavern, I glimpsed Maura and Carey sitting at another table with Mart drifting around nearby. It made sense, since this was the best pub in town. The New Moon was werewolf centred and at the mercy of the pack's notoriously terrible band on a nightly basis, while the Laughing Pixie was chiefly for students and had floors so sticky that you had to be careful not to leave your shoes behind when you walked in.

I did my best to ignore their presence and filled Nathan in on my dad's meeting with my foster parents, since I hadn't had the chance to tell him in person yet.

Nathan's brows shot up when I mentioned the man who'd dropped dead. "You didn't mention that earlier."

"Slipped my mind," I admitted. "He was a normal as far as I could tell. I didn't see anything magical around, and neither did my dad."

Nathan didn't look convinced. "I might have to look into that one later, just to see if there's a possible connection to the magical community. If your dad said otherwise, though, it's probably fine."

We moved on to other subjects, and I began to relax from the frazzled state our confrontation with Steve had put me in. At least I was until we were on our way out of the pub, when I caught a few words of Maura's conversation with the others.

"Look, it's easy enough," Maura was saying. "You don't have to come with us, Carey, but I won't be out of your sight for long anyway. Mart will be with you."

"But I want to come," he protested.

"Behave," Maura told him. "We'll meet at eleven or so when everyone is asleep."

I looked for Nathan, who'd already left the pub ahead of me, but he hadn't heard them. *What are they scheming?*

———

If I were sensible, I would have left Maura alone, but the nagging doubt lurked in the back of my mind throughout the evening until long after Nathan and I had gone to bed. If they were plotting something illegal, then I shouldn't get involved, but there was no harm in warning them off. Right?

In the end, Sky decided for me by lying on my chest until I had to sit up or else lose the ability to breathe.

I winced when his clawed feet dug into my chest. "What?"

"Miaow." He jabbed a paw at the window before springing off me.

Sitting upright, I peered through the glass. I didn't see anything odd outside, but when I checked the time, the clock was about to strike eleven. Aka, the exact time when Maura had been planning her nighttime jaunt.

"How did you know?" I whispered to Sky. "You weren't even around earlier."

"Miaow."

Honestly.

I glanced at Nathan, but he was sound asleep, and the hours he worked meant he generally needed to grab any sleep he could get. If I got in and out of the house without disturbing him, then it'd be a small miracle, but it wouldn't be the first time I'd had to take an unplanned trip while he was sleeping. He'd believe me without question if I told him the Elf King or the fairies had dragged me out of bed, but I didn't want to lie to my boyfriend, and besides, it was Nathan who'd have to deal with the fallout if Steve wound up in an even worse mood than usual. Trying to talk Maura out of whatever she was planning was a better idea than lying awake and regretting not acting, so I tugged on some clothes and quietly made for the stairs. After giving Sky a stroke to say thanks, I tiptoed down to the lower floor.

Nathan had given me a spare key to his house so I could let myself back in if he got dragged outside on patrol, but I'd rather he didn't wake up to find me in a cell. With my Seven Millimetre Boots active, I glided down the row of terraced houses and along the route to the main road. As expected, I spotted Maura and Carey with Mart drifting along behind them—and heading in the direction of the police station.

"Maura," I hissed. "What are you doing?"

"Taking matters into our own hands." She barely gave me a glance and didn't slow her pace. "We're just going to grab the relevant files and get out. No harm done."

"No harm done?" She had to be joking. "You know, I'm starting to see how you ended up collapsing an entire coven you weren't even a member of."

Mart howled with laughter. "She isn't wrong."

Maura shot me a disgruntled look. "Look, do you really want this case to go unsolved?"

"No, but there're other ways to get the information that don't involve antagonising Steve."

"He's just the kind of authority figure I hate," she said. "He's full of nothing but hot air and bluster."

"He can still lock you in a cell, Maura." Arguing with her was like trying to convince my cat to do something he didn't want to do, and I sensed a losing battle on the horizon.

"I can easily get out of a cell," she said. "Just as I can easily get into the police's records without being seen."

"However stealthy you think you are, I can guarantee it won't stop you from getting caught," I warned.

"It's not stealth. It's my Reaper skills," she said. "Not only can I walk through walls, but I can also make myself completely unseen. If necessary, I can literally walk in circles around Steve without him having a clue I'm there."

Walk through walls? Seriously? "Turning invisible isn't a guarantee that he won't hear you. Shifters have sharp senses."

"Not for Reapers," said Maura. "We're silent as the grave by definition."

"She is," Carey put in. "I've seen her in action."

Nothing I said would convince Maura otherwise, that

much was obvious. Part of me was tempted to go back to bed, but a bigger part was curious as to how her stealthy Reaper powers actually worked. Besides, if she got caught, then someone would have to help Carey deal with Steve's wrath, and who else would volunteer? Mart, being a ghost, was invisible to the entire police force.

All right. If their plan failed, I'd fetch Nathan and explain. If it worked, then I'd see if the file revealed anything more on our elusive ghost.

Maura stretched her hands out as if about to touch an invisible door. "I'm going in."

"Good luck," Carey whispered from beside me.

Darkness spread around Maura, the same way it had when she'd called on the ghost—but this time she disappeared into the blackness herself, as if the shadows had swallowed her whole.

My heart leapt into my throat. "Erm… is she okay?"

Carey nodded. "Yeah, she's a Reaper. The afterworld can't harm her."

Several long and tense seconds passed before Maura reappeared in a blur of shadow, a folder clutched in her hand. "See? No harm done."

"Don't speak too soon." That was it? I wouldn't lie, it felt kind of anticlimactic, and part of me expected to hear the roar of angry gargoyles and the beating of wings overhead. Though she still had to put the folder *back* after she'd read its contents.

Maura stepped forward, the shadows vanishing. "Let's see what Steve wanted to hide."

"I don't think he wanted to hide anything. He just wanted to keep us out of his hair," I replied. "Though I hope it was worth the risk anyway."

Maura opened the file. A single piece of paper fluttered to the ground, which she caught in her hand. Even from a distance, I could read the word printed across the top of the page: CLOSED. *Guess not, then.*

"She disappeared," Maura read from the page. "The police sent out search parties to look for her, but they ended up dropping the case."

"We already knew that, right?" So much for the file holding the answers. "They never found her body, presumably."

"It should be easy enough to confirm if we ask some of the other local ghosts," said Maura. "How far are we from the town's graveyard?"

I raised a brow. "First you want to break into the police station, now the graveyard?"

"Can't we just walk in?"

"Not unless you want to be cornered by the resident vampires," I replied. "And trust me, Samuel is positively harmless compared to the others."

"The vampires live next to the graveyard?" Carey's nose scrunched. "Why?"

"When there are vampires around, then the odds of dead people waking up increase dramatically," I explained. "That's the main reason they keep the gates locked."

"A locked gate is hardly an obstacle," said Maura.

How had I guessed she was going to say that? "At least

put the file back before you leap headlong into your next stunt."

Maura closed the file. "Fine."

Without further ado, she vanished into the shadows. Carey and I hardly had the chance to exchange glances before she was back, the file no longer in her hand. "You might as well have kept it. I doubt Steve would ever have noticed it was missing."

Whether I agreed with her plan or not, I'd hoped there'd be a tiny clue in the file we could use to identify the link between Mattie's ghost and the Shadow on the Lake. No such luck, but I wasn't sure the graveyard would be any different.

Maura glanced up at the gloomy midnight sky. "When does the graveyard open?"

"I think the vamps unlock the gates before they go to sleep around six or seven in the morning," I recalled. "You'll find them harder to evade than Steve, so I'd put that one on hold."

"Fine, I'll be good," Maura said. "We'll visit the graveyard in the morning. Meet you at seven."

Typical. "Fine, but you'd better hope the vampires are sleeping."

One thoroughly restless night later, my alarm went off at half past six, waking both Nathan and me. The real miracle was that Nathan hadn't woken up at all when I'd sneaked in and out, though he was used to the four cats we collectively owned climbing all over him in the middle of the night anyway.

"Where're you off to?" he asked groggily when I began fumbling around for my clothes.

Part of me wanted to snag an extra hour of sleep instead of accompanying Maura and the others on their latest ill-advised jaunt, but I dreaded to think what kind of mischief they'd create at the graveyard while I wasn't there. "I have to meet Maura."

"For what?" He blinked, waking up a little more. "I didn't think Reapers were morning people. What's she up to?"

I drew in a breath. "On a scale of one to ten, how annoyed would you be if I mentioned Maura used her stealthy Reaper powers to sneak in and out of the police's records last night?"

"She didn't." He sat bolt upright in bed. "Blair, please tell me she didn't."

"Sorry." I hung my head. "I meant to tell you when I came back from supervising, but you were dead to the world."

"That might end up being true in a literal sense if Steve finds out." He groaned. "Really, Blair? You couldn't talk her out of it?"

"I tried, but she was adamant that she could walk through the wall without making a sound. She was right." I finished putting on my clothes. "Reapers have some serious tricks up their sleeves. It took less than ten seconds for her to get in and out of there, and she replaced the file even quicker."

He swore under his breath. "Then she'd better hope nobody notices anything out of place in the records. Where are you going now then?"

"To stop them from getting into a similar level of

trouble with the vampires for sneaking into the graveyard to see if Mattie Lyons is buried there."

"Why would…" he trailed off. "Never mind. It's their funeral if they want Vincent to skewer them."

"Precisely my thinking, but the vamps are usually asleep by now, aren't they?"

"They'll wake up pretty quickly if they see a Reaper walking past their house."

That's what worries me. If I went with them, I could pretend I'd come to visit my mother's grave, though she wasn't actually buried there. Perhaps the same was true of Mattie, but there was no telling whether the ghosts in the graveyard would be able to give her any relevant information or not.

"Don't forget Vincent has helped us before," I reminded him. "He doesn't always answer my questions, but he isn't as much of a stubborn obstructionist as Steve is."

"I doubt threatening him with the Grim Reaper will go over well."

"I'll make sure she behaves." I kissed him goodbye before leaving the house. Once again, I wore my Seven Millimetre Boots in case I needed to make a quick getaway if our trip to the cemetery went sideways.

As promised, I met Maura and Carey at the top of the highest point in town, where the vampires' soot-coloured brick headquarters sat next to the graveyard. As usual, the blinds were down, preventing any daylight from getting through the windows. While vampires didn't burst into flames in the daylight like some legends said, they preferred to wander around at night and generally slept during the day. I kept my fingers crossed behind my back that they never noticed we were there.

"Are you floating?" Carey eyed my feet. "What kind of boots are those?"

"Seven Millimetre Boots," I replied. "Haven't you seen them before?"

"Hawkwood Hollow is a little out of touch with the rest of the paranormal world." Maura jogged over to the cemetery gate and nudged it open. "Perils of half the residents being dead. So, whereabouts will we be most likely to find Mattie's grave?"

"The witches bury their dead next to their fellow coven members, so she won't be with the Meadowsweet Coven." Other than that, the graveyard was extensive. I held my breath when Maura pushed the gate inward, but no vampires assailed us, and we walked in without being challenged.

We made our way past the neat rows of carved headstones marked with plaques which told us which coven or family their occupants belonged to. Stone mausoleums were designated for the bigger families, but Mattie hadn't been part of a major coven. Minutes trickled by as we covered row after row, examining each grave marker.

When we reached the end of the witches' part of the cemetery, I halted. "I don't think she's buried in here. Also, if I stay for much longer, I'm going to be late for work."

"We don't have much left to search." Maura scanned the area and pointed to our right. "What's over there?"

I peered at an overgrown signpost covered in so much moss that I couldn't read the words on it, but the arrow led us to a far corner of the cemetery I'd overlooked. Grass covered the cracked stones, the graves were worn away from neglect or age, and each plot was barren of any flowers for their occupants. A shiver of unease ran down my spine.

"Is that where they bury non-coven witches?" Carey looked up and down the row of graves.

"Found her." Ahead of me, Maura came to a halt next to a patch of grass marked with Mattie's name. "Doesn't look like she had any family."

The neighbouring graves didn't bear her family's name, and Mattie's grave stood alone. "You can't use your Reaper senses to see if she's buried here or not, can you?"

"No, but I can check on the local spirits to see if anyone's watching."

Darkness swathed her hands. Instead of a ghost, a sharp voice came from behind us instead. "Who is disturbing the dead?"

Carey gave a strangled scream, and Maura dropped the shadows. Despite recognising Vincent's voice, I startled, my heart plummeting below the ground to join the unfortunate souls beneath.

Movement flickered in the corner of my eye, and a dark figure stepped into view. Tall and pale and dressed in his customary funeral-appropriate attire, Vincent studied me for a moment before he turned his attention to my companions. His fangs showed when he spoke while addressing me. "Why did you bring a Reaper into our home, Blair Wilkes?"

My throat went dry. "Maura isn't a practising Reaper."

Maura herself glowered at him. "Would it matter if I wasn't? Everyone in here is already long gone."

Carey backed away from Mattie's grave, tripping over

her own feet in an effort to avoid the vampire. "Maura, come on. We should go."

Vincent ignored her and advanced on Maura. "Are you here on the orders of the Reaper Council, I wonder?"

"Definitely *not*," Maura responded.

Vincent smiled. "Then I imagine they'd appreciate it if I gave them a call and told them one of their Reapers seems to have gone astray."

"Hang on," I said, alarmed. "Maura's not here to start a feud with you. We're looking into the case of a witch who died a few years ago and whose ghost is haunting the lake. There seems to be some confusion over whether her body was ever recovered. The police records suggest not, but we wanted to see if her grave was here."

Vincent glanced at me. "Steve let you see the records, did he?"

"There wasn't anything to see, but her ghost has a reputation."

If I had to guess, he'd read the truth from my thoughts the instant he'd set eyes on me. I could sometimes block him from reading my mind but not when he sneaked up on me from behind, and it'd been a while since I'd last set eyes on the vampires' leader. Vincent was generally reclusive anyway, but these days, if I had a question that required a vampire's input, I asked Alissa to pass on word to Samuel instead.

Vincent studied me. "I didn't know you missed me that much, Blair."

"I'm out of practise at keeping you from reading my thoughts." At least with his attention on me, he'd momentarily taken his eyes off Maura. I had an inkling even he'd have trouble catching her if she used that shadow-jumping power of hers like she had beforehand. "Hang on. You were around when Mattie Lyons disappeared, right?"

"I can hardly be expected to remember every single person who dies," he said. "I have lived for a very long time."

"She only died a few years ago." I indicated her weed-strewn grave marker. Vincent was the mind reader, not me, so I had no way to tell if he was being truthful or not, but he was known for conveniently withholding information from me whenever he felt like it. "I imagine her ghost wants to move on to the next world, and the quickest way to achieve that is to give her closure."

"I wouldn't presume to guess the desires of a ghost," he replied. "They can be as complicated as the living are."

"She disappeared, and the police dropped the case, though," I said. "Does being buried here mean she had no coven at all? She was only eighteen, and I don't think she had any family."

She'd dropped out of the academy too. Put together with her grave's neglected state, I didn't blame her for sticking around to haunt people who'd ignored her in life *and* death. Did her frustration extend to deadly curses, though?

"I imagine she grew up in the care system and turned down any coven who tried to recruit her." Vincent's mouth turned down at the corners. "I can think of many others who fit the same mould."

A pang struck my heart. "I'm sure the people who knew her while she was alive would want to know her fate."

"Nevertheless, if you ask the ghosts who are resident to the cemetery, you're going to be disappointed. The ones who stay here tend to be too self-interested to care about other spirits."

"It was a long shot." I beckoned to the others. "Come on, we're better off talking to the living."

"Correct." Vincent gave Maura a withering look. "Do try to avoid leaving a mess behind, won't you?"

Before she could reply, he was gone in the blink of an eye. Carey gasped, while Maura simply watched the spot where he'd disappeared with an inscrutable expression.

"Do vampires generally have an issue with Reapers?" I asked. "Or just you?"

"I forgot about that slight issue." She grimaced. "Like I said, we don't have any resident vamps in Hawkwood Hollow, but they can get touchy about Reapers going near their territories."

I supposed immortals who'd risen from death would have a rivalry with people who reaped the souls of anyone who passed on. Since both vampires and Reapers were eternal and undying, then one would think they'd have more in common than not, but if my time in the paranormal world had taught me one thing, it was that the smallest differences could be the most divisive.

In any case, we'd hit a literal dead end, and the others didn't want to linger. Carey wore a relieved expression when we left the graveyard behind.

"Can you please try not to start any feuds while I'm at work?" I directed my question chiefly at Maura. "In fact, I'd be careful with Samuel too. I'm not sure he knew you were a Reaper when you first met."

"They're mind readers, though, aren't they?" asked Carey.

"Their abilities don't work on Reapers," Maura said.

"That might be one reason they aren't fond of us. I imagine Samuel would have guessed if he tried to probe into my thoughts when I first went in the library."

"He's less prone to using his powers on bystanders, but you'd better hope he's more tolerant of Reapers than Vincent is," I said. "Also, he can read *your* mind, Carey."

Carey eyed me. "Didn't you mention being able to keep Vincent out of your thoughts?"

"I had a few run-ins with the vampires when I first moved to town, and I don't like them being able to poke around in my head whenever they feel like it, so I learned to resist," I explained. "It doesn't always work though."

My magic gave me some measure of natural resistance as well, but I decided against telling Maura that. I was glad *she* wasn't a mind reader because she had far too many gifts at her disposal already.

"The library might be our best bet for finding out more information on Mattie," Maura said. "If she grew up in the care system, where will we be more likely to find out the details?"

"Honestly? I have no idea." I'd been fostered myself, but I'd grown up in the normal world's system, and I had no experience of the magical world's equivalent. "Try the library then."

"All right," she said. "Failing that, I'll go back to the lake and see if she's in a talkative mood this time."

Needless to say, I had considerable trouble concentrating at work, thanks to the lingering worries in the back of my mind that Maura would find a way to get herself into more trouble while I was gone. I had no doubts that she could even in the library, if it turned out that Samuel realised she was a Reaper. While he had little in common with Vincent, the fact that all vampires allegedly hated the Reapers on principle might throw yet another wrench into Maura's ghost-hunting plans.

Speaking of Samuel, I still needed to find him a suitable fairy assistant, and while I'd spoken to several promising candidates the previous day, I had yet to work out how they'd fit into the work environment. The best way to do that was to send them to the library in person, so I crossed my fingers behind my back that he wasn't currently engaged in an argument with Maura and called him on my work phone.

Samuel answered right away. "Who is it?"

"This is Dritch & Co."

"Blair." He sounded pleased. "Are you calling about my new assistant?"

"I have a few candidates, but I wondered if you might want to meet them in person before making a decision. There are three on the short list."

"Excellent," he said. "I think I will interview all of them in person, then. Send them my way at, say, noon."

Had he seen Maura yet? He must have if she'd gone straight there after leaving the cemetery, but every moment that he spent in her company risked his discovery that he'd let a Reaper into the library. He couldn't know, surely, unless he was either a spectacular actor or genuinely unbothered about her presence there.

"Should I come with them?" I suggested. "I mean, the campus is a complete maze, and I don't want them to get lost."

"How kind of you to offer," he said. "I look forward to meeting the candidates."

He ended the call, and I gave myself a mental shake. To be honest, it wasn't a terrible idea for me to accompany the fairies to the library. While the students who'd been angry about the fairies' presence in town had stopped being as vocal since their public humiliation, that didn't mean the candidates wouldn't draw attention if they all entered the campus at once. But it also didn't mean my boss would be as keen on the idea, of course.

When I rose to my feet, Bethan glanced up from her work. "Where are you going, Blair?"

"To ask the boss a question."

I hoped Veronica would be in an accommodating mood. I never quite knew what to expect from her, and while it was sometimes possible to glean her mood from the theme of her office décor, that wasn't always the case. Today's theme turned out to be abstract art. Bright paintings of random shapes hung from the walls, and the furniture had been replaced with what appeared to be blocks of wood.

"Blair," she said when I perched awkwardly on one of the blocks that vaguely resembled an upside-down chair. "How are you getting on?"

"Good," I replied. "I managed to find some people who might be suited to work as Samuel's assistant, and he'd like them to go to the library to interview in person."

"Excellent," she said. "What did you want to ask me, then?"

"I wondered if I could escort them there in case they get lost." I faltered. "Also, there have been incidents with the students and the fairies before, and I think it'll put them at ease if I go there with them. The interviews start at noon."

"That's a good idea, Blair," she said. "Noon, you say? You can make up the lost time during your lunch hour."

"Sure." At least that assuaged my guilt at being slightly less than truthful with my boss, though I was sure I'd made the right call. Only one of the three candidates had been to the campus before: Ani, a friend of mine who'd once had a habit of pranking the students. Maybe they did need my supervision even if Maura didn't.

After the other candidates had replied to my invitation to meet Samuel in person, I set off for the library just before noon. The vampire librarian was pretty hard-core, so anyone who wanted to interview as his assistant would need to know what they were getting into. It wasn't a terrible idea to give them a trial run first, though I hoped Maura wouldn't derail the whole thing.

Not that I thought she'd actually get into a brawl with Samuel if he found out she was a Reaper, but you never knew.

The three candidates waited outside the campus gates as we'd arranged. Of the three, only Ani had dressed appropriately, in a shirt and a pair of trousers that looked slightly too big for her, as if she'd borrowed them from someone else. Her white-blond hair puffed out like a cloud, but she was still considerably more presentable than the other two—one of whom wore what appeared to be a tutu and a knitted cap, and the other who was dressed in a heavy overcoat that smelled vaguely of mould. *Oh boy.*

"Hey, Blair." Ani gave a nervous glance over her shoulder. "I'm glad you're coming with us. I nearly got hit by a flying carpet just then."

So the students had managed to rescue it from the roof after all. "Yeah, I'd keep an eye out for low-flying broomsticks as well. This is why I generally recommend walking across campus instead of flying, even though it's slower."

I found myself glad I'd offered to escort the students, since on our journey to the library, we had to dodge a number of fox shifters, avoid being hit by spells miscast by duelling wizards, and even run from a rampaging herd of cattle.

"Where'd they come from?" Ani doubled over to catch her breath.

"A spell, probably." From the way the other two contenders held their arms over their heads as if they expected to get hit by projectiles, they wouldn't last long working here without a nervous breakdown even if Samuel kindly overlooked their inability to read the dress code I'd sent to them.

Upon reaching the library, I opened the door and ushered the others ahead of me into the relative safety of the maze of bookshelves. Samuel emerged from the nearest, eyeing my oddly dressed companions. "Blair. Have you decided on a change of employment?"

"No, I brought your interviewees." He was *probably* joking, but I felt the need to clarify the matter. "We just about got here in one piece."

"Then I appreciate your noble effort." After raising his brows at the others' strange fashion choices, he beckoned to Ani. "Come with me."

I nodded encouragingly to Ani, who at least looked less terrified than the other two. While she followed Samuel between the shelves, I caught sight of Maura and Carey sitting at the same table as they had before. They'd stacked the newspaper articles into a few piles around a large piece of blank paper, on which they appeared to be in the process of drawing a map.

Carey looked up and caught my eye. "Blair, I thought you were at work."

"I'm supervising interviewees for Samuel's new assistant." My gaze slid to the paper, which depicted a lopsided shape that resembled a giant blob. "What's that?"

"A self-portrait," Mart answered.

"Ha ha," said Maura. "Our research into the foster system hit a dead end, so we tried another tack. I'm drawing a map of the lake so I can mark out all the places the ghost has been sighted. That way, we can narrow down where her body might be located."

"Would moving her body encourage her to move on?" I queried.

"It might," said Maura. "In her case, it seems likely that it'll be enough. She's not out for revenge, I don't think. She just wants people to know she's there."

I'd had the impression she'd rather we left her alone, but that was to be expected given that Maura had unexpectedly disturbed her rest. "You're the expert."

Drawing a map was an improvement from starting arguments with vampires, so I left them to it and returned to wait with the other two interviewees. The slight problem was they'd both disappeared. I peered behind the shelves, wondering if they'd got lost, but Samuel soon reappeared with a windswept-looking Ani in tow. "Ah, Blair. I believe we are short on candidates."

"I don't know where they went," I said apologetically. "I'm not sure either of them would be the right fit anyway."

"I have to agree." He indicated Ani, who was attempting to flatten her blond hair. "Fortunately, this fine candidate…"

"Ani," she ventured.

"Ani is perfect for my needs," he finished. "I have invited her to do a trial for the rest of the day."

"Oh?" I studied Ani's expression, surprised that she'd readily agreed to work on campus after the prior unpleasantness with a handful of students. "Did you say yes?"

"I did." Her face hardened in a determined expression. "I'm going to give it a shot."

"Let's begin," he called to her. "No time to waste."

He vanished in a single step, leaving the books on the shelves rattling in his wake. Ani took a startled step back.

"Are you sure about this?" I whispered to her. "He's like this all the time."

"I gathered." She gave a wry smile. "On balance, it's better than working for the town's security team. I heard Steve yelling at them earlier."

Hoping it hadn't been Nathan he'd shouted at, I decided to leave them to it. "You'll be able to find your way out again when the trial's over?"

"If all else fails, I'll fly over the fence."

"All right." Barely half an hour had passed, but at least I wouldn't have to work straight through my lunch break if I went back to the office now.

As I made for the door, Maura crossed the library to overtake me, her hand-drawn map tucked under her arm and Carey hurrying to keep up with her.

"Maura." I quickened my pace and followed her outside. "If you were plotting to do anything dangerous or potentially illegal again, would you tell me?"

"Dangerous?" she echoed. "I wouldn't classify anything we've done so far as particularly dangerous."

Mart snorted. "You'd say the same if we'd been chased by a monster from the afterworld."

I had no idea if he was implying that they'd actually met a monster of some kind from the afterworld, but I imagined I'd be better off not knowing the details. "Have you spoken to the ghost today?"

"That was next on the agenda," said Maura.

"I thought we were getting lunch," said Carey.

"We can do both." Maura walked through the campus, seemingly oblivious to the chaotic obstacles in our way. "I can't get any further with the map if I don't ask the ghost for more details on how she ended up in that lake."

"You really think she'll listen to you this time around?" For all we knew, dragging her past out into the open would cause her to clam up entirely, but I was out of any better ideas. Besides, revisiting the grumpy spirit was considerably less risky than going back to the graveyard or the police station. "She's not used to people waking her up to bombard her with questions, I'll bet."

Maura sidestepped a low-flying carpet. "I won't push her. I'll try to be tactful."

"You don't know the meaning of the word," Mart contributed.

From what I'd seen, he had a point there. "So you admit you might have been a bit hasty last time?"

Maura cast a disgruntled look at her brother. "I assumed we were dealing with a spirit who liked to terrorise people, not a lonely teenager."

Right. I'd assumed Maura's bluntness was typical of a Reaper, but she seemed to treat the living the same way as she did the dead.

"So you're going to ask nicely instead of dragging her out of her peaceful afterlife?" I asked.

"It's not peaceful," she murmured. "Hauntings aren't driven by spirits who are content to stay in their graves, and ghosts who choose that path are generally disturbed or dissatisfied at best. They want to move on, even if they don't know it yet."

Vincent had claimed otherwise, but I sensed that it wouldn't be wise to bring up the leading vampire again. We were lucky it hadn't come to an all-out fight between the pair of them earlier.

Since I'd be working through my lunch break, I bought a sandwich from the local café when the others stopped to buy lunch on the way to the lake. When we reached the shores of the glittering silver water, Maura and Carey sought out the same spot where the ghost had appeared the last time they'd encountered her. The still waters of the lake faced us, a deceptively calm sight compared to the shadows of the afterworld that sprang to Maura's hands.

Maura peered into the darkness. "Mattie? Are you there?"

The ghost didn't appear, but her disembodied voice shouted, "Didn't I tell you to go away?"

A rush of wind swept my hair back right before an invincible force grabbed my legs and dragged me towards the lake. I flailed, too startled to unfurl my wings before I hit the water and sank under. Surfacing, I gasped for air, treading water as I struggled to get my bearings. The ghost had somehow dragged me at least a hundred metres out, past the shallows and into deeper water. *How is that possible?*

"Blair?" Carey's eyes were round as saucers as she raised her wand. "Hang on, I'll get you out."

"No need." I kicked my way to the shallows and dragged myself onto the bank, sinking onto the grass to catch my breath. My hair was plastered to my head, and my clothes were sopping wet, but it could have been much worse. Lifting my head, I glared at the patch of darkness in front of Maura. "Not cool, Mattie. I wasn't the one who woke you up."

Maura dragged her eyes away from the darkness. "What happened to you?"

"Did you not see the ghost throw me into the lake?"

Maura gave me a baffled look. "The ghost isn't even here. She yelled at me and disappeared."

"She threw me over there." I pointed vaguely at the lake. "I don't see any other spirits, do you?"

Going back to work while dripping wet wasn't appealing, so I used a drying spell. It worked on my face and hair, but my clothes remained damp and uncomfortable. Another unwelcome thought hit me, and I dug in my pocket for my phone and found it dead. "Oh, come on."

"Let me fix that." Carey held out a hand. "I had to do the same to my laptop when one of the customers at the restaurant spilled Coke all over it."

For the lack of a better idea, I handed over my phone. "I didn't know you worked at a restaurant."

"My mum runs the Riverside Inn, and I help out at the restaurant sometimes." She nodded to Maura. "Maura works there full-time now."

"So hunting ghosts isn't your main job?"

"No." A muscle twitched in Maura's jaw. "Ghosts don't tend to pay well. Also, I don't think she's coming back."

"Then I vote we get away from the lake before someone else falls in." Frankly, I was more concerned for my poor phone than my damp work clothes. I didn't have a ton of spare cash lying around. "I have a co-worker who's good with technology, but I don't know if she's ever fixed a phone that went for a swim before."

"I can fix it." Carey held the phone in one hand and pointed her wand at it with the other. A jet of water shot out of the end and soaked me all over again. "Oops."

Mart laughed openly while Maura stifled a grin. I glowered at her. "If your ghost has cost me my phone, then you can pay for a new one."

"Hey, I didn't ask her to throw you into the lake," she protested. "Also, I'm not sure it was even her."

"How many other hostile ghosts are in the lake?" I folded my arms across my chest. "Maybe the reason she has a reputation for cursing people is because of annoying ghost hunters who won't leave her alone."

"There you go." Carey pushed my phone in front of my nose. To my astonishment, the screen had come back on again, as if it had suffered no damage at all.

"Huh." I took the phone and clicked the home button. It worked. "Thanks."

"No lasting damage," Maura observed with a satisfied nod. "See?"

"If we're all cursed, I'll make sure she takes you first."

"Fair enough." She took a decisive step away from the lake. "I'm going back to the library. You?"

"I have to get back to work." Her willingness to turn her back on the ghost struck me as suspicious to say the least, however. "You're giving up on the lake?"

"No, I'm changing strategies." She gave me an assessing look. "Are you absolutely certain you didn't see anyone else when you fell into the lake? Living or dead?"

"You're the Reaper, not me," I retaliated. "What, you think there's more than one ghost?"

"I think there's a strong possibility."

On that ominous note, it was time to return to work. While she and Carey left, I made my way to Dritch & Co's office. As luck would have it, I found Veronica chatting to Callie in the reception area.

When she saw me come in, Veronica remarked, "I wasn't aware going to the library involved going underwater."

My face heated. "It was an accident. Didn't have time to change afterwards."

"I think I might try an underwater theme in my office next." She looked me up and down. "Try not to drip on the paperwork, won't you?"

"I won't." Gathering the remnants of my dignity, I returned to the main office.

"Blair," said Bethan. "What did you do? Go for a swim?"

Of all the days for it *not* to be raining outside. At least then I'd have a reasonable excuse for the state of my clothes. "Ran into a backfiring spell on campus."

"The interview went well then?"

"One of them did. The other candidates took off."

Bethan's brow wrinkled. "Intimidated, were they?"

"I think so. Plus they didn't quite get the dress code requirements, so the candidate Samuel picked was definitely the best choice."

"That's good news," said Rob. "Now you're back, you can help us with this mountain of paperwork."

"I can hardly wait."

At least I couldn't get into too much trouble while sitting behind a desk, though it was hard to keep Maura and the ghost from my thoughts. Why had *I* been the one she'd thrown into the lake? Granted, since Maura was a Reaper, maybe she was immune from that kind of mischief anyway, but frankly, I wasn't sure that being tossed into the water herself would put Maura off.

If there was more than one ghost, though, which one had thrown me into the water? And which was the source of the rumours?

Nathan met me after work and greeted me with a kiss and a raised brow at my wrinkled shirt. "Hey, Blair. Why are you all damp?"

"I had a run-in with the ghost earlier."

His brows shot up. "At work?"

"No, I unwisely decided to go to the lake with Maura again on my lunch break. The ghost didn't take kindly to being disturbed and threw me in."

"I didn't know ghosts could do that."

"Most can't." I walked alongside him down the street. "Unless it was a manifestation of the curse, but I don't see why it'd hit me and not the others."

"Curse?" he echoed. "What curse?"

"According to legend, people who disturb the ghost who lives near the lake often meet an unfortunate end." A shiver ran down my spine that wasn't entirely due to my earlier soaking. "Which is what allegedly happened to the guy who wrote the article on the ghost that led Maura here in the first place."

"The ghost *killed* him?" Scepticism underlaid his tone.

"No, he crashed his car. Same difference, supposedly." I shrugged, trying to ignore the unease prickling across my shoulder blades. "All three of us set eyes on the ghost, and nothing weird has happened until today, but being thrown into the lake isn't the same as being cursed to meet one's doom."

"Maura is more of a menace than any ghost," he said. "It shouldn't surprise me that she's cavalier about her own safety when it comes to ghosts, given that she's a Reaper, but I'm surprised she'd put a teenage girl in harm's way as well."

"Carey came here voluntarily. In fact, I'm pretty sure it was her idea." Which didn't mean it was safe, but she clearly trusted Maura a great deal. "Anyway, she thinks there's more than one ghost involved. Does Steve have you patrolling tonight?"

"Unfortunately, yes. That's why I came to see you now."

I pulled a face. "I bet that's payback for the way I annoyed him yesterday."

"It'd have been worse if he knew your friend had broken into the records." He spoke in a low voice. "By the way, I had a bit of time to look up that man who died last weekend."

I tripped mid-step, catching my balance before I fell. "Wait, you did? Did you find anything weird?"

"Nothing magical," he replied. "But his death was reported in the normals' news and not ours despite him being a wizard."

"He was a wizard?" That increased the odds of his death having a magical cause, but since he'd died surrounded by normals, perhaps nobody had made the connection yet.

"Exactly," he said. "Fairy Falls is the nearest magical community to the location where he died, but he's not from here. Considering we can barely get Steve to focus on crimes that actually *are* local…"

"Then the odds of him helping in this one are about as high as him developing a passion for line dancing," I finished.

"Exactly." Nathan's gaze dropped to my pocket as my phone buzzed. "I think someone's calling you."

"That or it's broken after all." I fished my phone out of my pocket and found Mr Wilkes's name flashing across the top of the screen. "Nah, my foster parents are calling me. See you later?"

"Sure." Nathan checked the time. "I'd better head over to the police station, but I'll message you in a bit."

As he departed, I answered the phone. "Hey, Dad."

"Blair," said Mr Wilkes. "How're you?"

"I'm fine. Just leaving the office." Doubly glad that my phone had escaped a watery grave, I veered towards home. "You?"

"Good, except our car broke down earlier in the middle of a busy road."

My heart jolted. "Seriously?"

"It's been stalling all week, so it isn't really surprising, but we got lucky," he replied. "We've also had a few annoying accidents at home. Nothing new, really. How many times have we had to fix the plumbing on this old house?"

"I lost count at a dozen." While it might be refreshing to hear about mundane disasters to take my mind off everything else, the car incident reminded me of the unfortunate ghost hunter who'd written that article.

"A roof tile nearly fell on my head earlier as well."

"Be careful," I told him. "Thought I was supposed to be the accident-prone one."

"Yes, I remember." He chuckled. "Not just you, but anyone who got near you as well. Like that time you turned off all those computers at your office."

"Ha." That kind of disaster was rarer now that I understood my fairy-witch nature, but my foster parents didn't have the same barriers hindering them from interacting with the world at large. They'd entirely forgotten their brief and unpleasant experience with the magical world, after all.

"Anyway, talk soon," he said.

"Bye." I ended the call, trying to quell my sense of unease. The odds that my foster parents had stepped into the backlash of a lucky latte's spell were slim enough to be nonexistent, and sometimes accidents just happened without any need for there to have been any magical interference.

Granted, when I'd discovered the magical world, I'd also found out that what I'd come to think of as my own personal bad luck curse had turned out to be a combination of my fairy magic and the glamour hiding my real appearance, which did not play well with technology. My foster parents, however, were utterly ordinary in every way.

The poor man who'd died, though? Nathan had said he was a wizard, and I'd forgotten to ask for the guy's name. Since I didn't have a magic lesson this evening and Steve had sunk my hopes of a date with Nathan, I had a little time to do some research of my own.

I got back to my flat to find that Alissa was out, presumably at work. Sky always seemed to know whose house I was going to walk into at any given time because he waited expectantly by the food bowls. After changing out of my damp work clothes and putting out some food for the cats, I settled down on the sofa and loaded up the Wizarding Web on my phone. I'd need to start with the normal world's news sites, unless the magical world had picked up on the story by this point. Someone must know who he was, surely.

I tried several variations of "man drops dead in cafe in Sloan" before I found what I was looking for. A smaller magical newspaper had reported the news, giving the man's name as Leroy Quint. When I ran a search, I had to scroll through several pages of junk before I encountered the words "Leroy Quint: ghost hunter."

The phone slid from my grip, landing on Sky, who swatted it away with a disgruntled meow. Heart thumping, I retrieved my phone and tapped on the link. Leroy Quint, it seemed, had made a living travelling around and visiting haunted locations, and while the article I'd opened didn't specify his next destination, I could hazard a guess.

Closing down the tab, I turned to my cat, who looked at me with unblinking eyes. "Unless I'm mistaken, this is the second ghost hunter who's allegedly died after looking for the Shadow on the Lake."

"Miaow" was Sky's response.

"I'll tell her," I decided. "Maura, I mean. I probably should have mentioned the dead guy when we first met, but I'd never have guessed he was a ghost hunter. I didn't even know he was magical."

Sky simply curled up on the sofa and yawned. "Miaow."

Leaving him to sleep, I grabbed my coat and shoes and left the flat. I figured Maura would likely have gone back to the lake, and as reluctant as I was to take another swim, it seemed only fair to warn her of the latest development.

My guess turned out to be right, and I was halfway to the lake when I spied Maura heading in the same direction. Upon seeing my approach, she came to a halt. "Hey."

"No luck finding the ghost?" I asked.

"No, but you look like you saw a ghost yourself," said Maura. "What happened?"

I drew in a breath. "I don't know if you heard, but a man died near Fairy Falls the day you showed up in town. Turns out he was a ghost hunter. What're the odds?"

Her eyes rounded. "A ghost hunter? Was he here to look for the Shadow on the Lake?"

"I don't know, but I find it difficult to believe it's a coincidence," I said. "He was called Leroy Quint. A wizard. He died in a normal town, so the news of his death hasn't spread that far in the magical world yet. I saw him not long before he died, and he was acting strangely, as if he could see something nobody else could."

"Not a ghost?" Carey gave Maura an uneasy look, but she appeared as unruffled as ever.

"I'd have been able to see if there'd been a ghost around," I reminded her. "But he seemed to drop dead out of nowhere. No obvious cause."

"Whereabouts did he die?" asked Maura.

"Sloan," I replied. "It's a normal town, which is why I

didn't realise there might be a connection until I found out his name and did some digging."

A thoughtful expression crossed her face. "Weird, that. I've never heard his name, but I can't say I've met many ghost hunters either."

I debated asking if she'd chased off the competition, but I decided against it. The poor guy had seemed pretty freaked out before his death. Had there been a ghost somewhere outside the shopping centre that I hadn't seen?

"If he died after seeing the Shadow on the Lake..." Carey faltered. "Maybe this isn't a good idea. Looking for the body, I mean. Mattie might get mad at us."

"Was that your plan?" I asked.

Maura inclined her head. "Yeah. I figured if we could find her body and inform the authorities so she can be properly buried, it might help her settle down."

"What about your theory of there being more than one ghost?"

"I don't have any substantial evidence," she answered. "Only instinct and the fact that Mattie Lyons's behaviour doesn't match the Shadow on the Lake's reputation."

"No..." Carey chewed on her lower lip. "I don't think she's the one who threw Blair into the lake."

I felt a surge of unexpected pity for Carey. She couldn't be older than sixteen or so, and she had none of the advantages of being a Reaper, not even the ability to see ghosts. She must trust Maura to not endanger her, but there was a limit to how a Reaper could keep an ordinary teenager safe from paranormal dangers that had zero effect upon Maura herself.

"What about those two dead ghost hunters?" I reminded her.

"There's no real proof the ghost killed either of them," Maura said. "Besides, we only have one full day left to look for the ghost. If we don't get back to Hawkwood Hollow when we planned, Allie will show up looking for us."

"Who's Allie?"

"Carey's mother."

I raised a brow. "She entrusted you with looking after her, did she?"

"Yes, and don't look at me like that. I didn't put her in danger, and she came here with full understanding of what she was getting into."

I had the impression I'd be arguing with a brick wall if I insisted otherwise, so I changed the subject. "Have you considered talking to some of the people who knew Mattie when she was alive?"

That was inadvisable given Maura's temperament, but not compared to angering a ghost who might have killed two living people.

"Given that I'm not local, I didn't get very far with my research," she responded. "But I'm sure there's more to the girl's death than the public records show. I don't think she died by accident."

"You think she was murdered." And… what? Someone had covered it up? "Unless you want to admit we sneaked a look at Steve's files, they won't believe we just stumbled upon that conclusion."

"Not necessarily," said Maura. "I can say I talked to the ghost, and *she* told me they stopped trying to find her body."

"They won't take the word of a ghost as proof," I said. "Not even from a Reaper."

"I've heard *that* one before." Her eyes narrowed. "Look, we're never going to have ideal conditions to expose this ghost. If I've learned anything from dealing with spirits, sometimes you have to keep digging into the past even when people start trying to take away the spade."

I wasn't entirely convinced that would be enough to work on Steve, whose usual policy for people digging into the past was to grab the spade and thwack them on the head with it, but Maura had already demonstrated she didn't fear him in the slightest.

Never mind Steve, though. Was anything worth risking the wrath of a bloodthirsty ghost?

My phone buzzed with a message from Nathan confirming that he'd be patrolling all evening. I replied saying I didn't mind staying at home with Alissa, though I was starting to wonder if it'd require both of our efforts to convince Maura to drop this ill-advised quest.

"We're going to the Troll's Tavern later if you want to join us," Maura offered. "We can talk more then."

"I'll ask Alissa to join us when she's home from work in an hour."

In truth, I was curious to find out if her scepticism about the Shadow on the Lake's curse extended to *two* people dropping dead shortly after visiting the lake. And whether she believed Mattie was truly part of the legend or simply an unlucky teenager who'd lingered past her time.

———

Alissa stood firm. "I can guarantee it wasn't the ghost who killed either of them," she said. "This Leroy Quint guy was unlucky, yeah, but he died in a normal town, right?"

"Yeah, but he was a wizard. And ghost hunter," I said. "Also, I might add that the ghost flung me into the lake earlier."

"So that's why your clothes are all wrinkled."

I scowled. "Sky, back me up."

Sky didn't so much as stir from his nap.

Alissa snorted. "Look, Blair, I have no doubt the ghost threw you in the lake, but there's a difference between that and killing two people who were nowhere near the scene of her haunting. What does Maura think?"

"Maura wants to find the ghost's real body and return it to her grave," I told her. "Give her a proper burial."

"Not a bad idea."

"No, but her alternative plan involves telling Steve her theory that someone intentionally gave up on investigating Mattie's death."

"That's a terrible one."

"I know, but it seems bizarre that nobody seems to have known her when she was alive," I said. "She grew up in the foster system, so I don't think Maura was able to get far with her research, but there must be someone we can talk to. Better than antagonising her ghost again."

"You've got that right," said Alissa. "All right, we'll talk through our options at the pub. If they have one day left before they leave town, then we can see to it that they don't get up to any more mischief."

"Fair point."

We left the flat and walked to the pub, where Maura and Carey waited for us near the door. When we picked out a table and sat down, Maura reached into her bag and pulled out her hand-drawn map.

"What is that?" Alissa peered at the blob-like drawing of the lake, which bore a slight resemblance to one of the abstract art pieces in Veronica's office. "A cloud?"

"A map, of course." Maura spread the sheet of paper across the table. "Of the lake."

"What're those?" I pointed at the X marks she'd scrawled at various intervals around the lake.

"Places the ghost has been sighted, according to the articles we found in the library," she replied. "None of those spots are anywhere near where we found the ghost ourselves."

"You think her body might be located at one of those spots?"

"Maybe, but it's not consistent." She poked a particular spot where several Xs overlapped. "The majority of reports say the ghost typically appears in this area, so it's our best bet."

"Except she usually comes out at midnight," Carey added.

When our food appeared on the table, Maura rolled up the map and put it away. "I've gone through all the articles, so to find out more, we'll have to go back to the lake."

"I thought you could use your Reaper abilities to find her at any time, not just midnight," Alissa commented.

"I can," she answered. "In theory. However, if there *is* more than one ghost, it would explain the discrepancies between our experience with Mattie and the ghost from the stories."

"So what's the plan?" I asked. "Go to the spot where

the ghost has been seen the most frequently at midnight and see who shows up?"

Maura picked up her fork. "It's that or find out where she grew up. I only found the name of one care home in town… Fairfield House?"

"Yes, it's run by the coven." Alissa nodded. "And owned by Madame Grey."

"Mattie wasn't a coven member, though." I picked up my own fork, though I didn't have much of an appetite.

"It's for all orphaned witches and wizards, not just coven members," Alissa responded. "They might be willing to talk to you, but you'll have to wait until tomorrow to pay them a visit."

"Thought so," Maura said. "We have one full day left after today, so ideally, we need to make the most of tonight. I think we should check out this haunted spot."

"At midnight," added Carey.

I frowned. "You think that by following the stories, you might be able to get through to her?"

"I've had worse ideas."

She wasn't wrong. "If it turns out Mattie isn't the Shadow on the Lake and you run into the real deal, then you're setting yourself up to end up like those two ghost hunters."

Maura made a sceptical noise. "I highly doubt the ghost *killed* them. There's such a thing as a coincidence."

"Alissa said the same." I turned to her teenage friend. "Carey, what do you think?"

"Don't try to sway her," Maura reprimanded me. "She doesn't scare as easily as you'd think."

Carey glanced at Maura. "I think we should give it a

shot. If the ghost is dangerous, then it won't be more than a Reaper can handle."

Maura gave a nod. "Exactly."

Neither Leroy Quint nor the unfortunate article writer had been a Reaper, but that didn't make it any less of a risk for those of us who didn't have that advantage.

Mattie's neglected grave came to mind again. Maybe everyone had forgotten her death, and haunting the living was her only remaining pastime. If we could do some small thing to help her, then we might as well see if she was truly the ghost from the legends.

"This is a one-off," Maura told me. "Afterwards, I'll go to another town to annoy someone else."

I gave a wry smile. Her self-awareness almost made up for her habit of making trouble, I had to admit. "All right, I'm in."

9

This time around, Sky didn't need to prod me awake at midnight. I was already awake, ready for one last ghost hunt. After getting dressed— picking out clothes that I didn't mind getting soaked if I took another swim in the lake—I pulled on my Seven Millimetre Boots and tiptoed out of the flat so as not to wake Alissa.

The moon hung low above the rooftops as I walked, finding Maura and the others waiting near the lake. In the darkness, the lake's surface resembled a glittering black slab extending into the distance and merging with the night sky.

"Hey," Maura said. "I've memorised the route to the right place, so we don't have to keep checking the map."

"Good, because your map is bloody awful," Mart told her. "I could draw better than that, and I can barely hold a pencil."

"Watch it, you." Maura turned her attention to the lake's surface. "The plan is to go to the place where the ghost is more likely to show her face. If she doesn't, then I can have a look around the area and see if her body is nearby."

"So now we're grave robbing by a lake instead of a graveyard."

"It's not grave robbing if she isn't buried in a grave."

"Technicalities." I rolled my eyes. "If you're certain you don't mind fishing a corpse out of a lake, then by all means, go ahead."

I hadn't told Nathan about our plan, though maybe I should have. He was patrolling tonight himself, but he didn't need to worry about Maura's antics on top of dealing with Steve's attitude problems. If we *did* find Mattie's body, then even Steve would have to stand up and take notice, but if the police had gone this long without finding her, then the odds were against us.

Our group followed the path southward alongside the lake until we left the town's boundaries behind. From there, we continued around the lower curve of the lake's surface. Outside of Fairy Falls, we were no longer in danger of trespassing on anyone's territory… except for the ghost's, that was. For that reason, I kept my Seven Millimetre Boots switched on so that I could maintain some control over my feet if an incorporeal force decided to throw me in the lake again.

"How will we know when we've reached the right spot?" I indicated the black stretch of the lake. "It all looks the same in the dark."

"Without any trees in the way, the ghost should be easy to spot." Maura walked on, not slowing down despite the slippery mud bordering the lake's edge.

"What's your plan if her body is buried in the middle of the lake?" I queried.

"I thought the lake was full of merpeople," she said. "Wouldn't they notice a body in the water?"

"Yes, but the lake is huge, and it's been years."

If her ghost had a favourite spot to haunt, it was somewhere to start, but my already flagging optimism faded even further as the minutes trickled by.

Finally, Maura came to a halt. "Here we are."

I shivered a little as a breeze stirred the surface of the water. "I don't see anything."

Maura turned on the spot, squinting across the water. "Neither do I."

"Well, I *feel* something," Mart announced. "And it's like someone walked on my grave. Don't any of you feel it?"

"Considering you're the only one of us who *has* a grave, no, we don't." Maura trod closer to the lake. "I wonder…"

The merest trace of shadows stirred around her hands, and a sudden flicker of light appeared against the lake's black surface. All the hairs on my arms stood up when a faint outline of a figure appeared in the distance, too far off for us to be able to make out its features.

"That isn't Mattie," Carey whispered, her face chalk white. "Maura… we should step back."

Maura didn't budge, but Mart did, and when the ghost began to glide towards us across the water, my blood iced over. The ghost definitely wasn't the same as the young woman we'd seen on the other side of the lake. It barely resembled a person at all, in fact, aside from the long, tangled hair hanging in curtains on either side of its—her —face. She was female, I was pretty sure, despite the inhuman hissing noise that escaped her as she faced our group.

An invisible blow slammed into all three of us, knocking us off our feet. Even my boots weren't enough to keep me from being flipped over and landing in a sprawling heap on the bank. Lifting my head, I saw Maura had landed several feet away, and Carey—something had grabbed her by the legs, dragging her into the water.

"Carey!" Maura yelled.

Carey screamed, flailing above the lake's surface. I scrambled in my pocket for my wand and cast a levitating spell, but the spell missed.

Maura vanished, leaping into the darkness. A heartbeat later, she appeared above the lake, grabbing Carey by the shoulders. Was she *standing* on the water? She must be, but the ghost wouldn't let go of her prey that easily. Maura tugged Carey, and the ghost tugged back.

"Let go of her!" Maura snarled.

I waved my wand again. My second levitating spell hit its mark, and Carey flew free of the ghost's grip. Unfortunately, the spell also caused Maura's grip to break, and Carey flew wildly towards the shore.

Maura vanished in a flash of shadow and emerged on the bank in time to steady Carey before the ghost could grab her again. "Are you okay?"

"Yeah." Carey sank breathlessly to the ground. "Thanks."

"Where—?" Maura spun on her heel and swore loudly. "She's gone."

The ghost had vanished as swiftly as she'd arrived, leaving no traces. I couldn't say I was sorry to see her gone. "C'mon, we'd better get out of here before she comes back."

"Not likely." Maura advanced on the lake. "You'd better not lay a finger on her again, do you hear me?"

"Maura." For all her skills—and walking on top of the shadowy water as if it was solid was apparently one of them—Carey had barely escaped the ghost's clutches. We didn't need to tempt fate.

"Maura," Carey called out in a tremulous voice. "Get back over here."

Mart was nowhere to be seen, I noticed belatedly, but he wouldn't have been able to help Carey escape. Ghosts couldn't touch the living… or so I'd thought.

Maura turned her back on the spot where the ghost had disappeared. "I can't even sense her in the afterworld anymore."

"I'm taking a wild guess it was *her* who dragged me into the lake earlier," I added. "Which is pretty unusual for a ghost, right?"

"She wasn't a regular ghost," Maura said. "I'll have to think way back to my Reaper training to figure out what she is. Where'd Mart go?"

"Here, but not for long." Mart reappeared at her shoulder. "In fact, now is a spectacular time for us to go home."

"Agreed," I said firmly. "That ghost we saw must be the real Shadow on the Lake, which means finding Mattie's body won't help us get rid of her."

"Right." Maura glared across the lake. "If she only appears at midnight, we'll have to wait until tomorrow night to have another chance."

"Another chance?" Carey's face shone pale under the moonlight. "You can't come back here."

"I'm not bringing you with me next time," said Maura. "Or anyone else either."

"Meaning me?" I gave her a challenging stare. "What if she's beyond your Reaper abilities?"

"She has a point." Mart jabbed a finger at her. "You don't have a scythe, remember? You can't just stick your blade in her and be done with it."

"I don't care," Maura answered. "She hurt Carey. As far as I'm concerned, that's reason enough to unleash my inner Reaper on her next time around. Besides, I've dealt with worse."

"Then leave me out of this," Mart said. "Some of us aren't built for mortal peril."

"You're already dead, Mart," said Maura.

Mart glowered at her. "You of all people know that being dead doesn't mean I can't be in danger."

"That means you should logically be more scared of *me* than the ghost."

Mart snorted. "Obviously I'm terrified of you. Mostly I'm scared of your lack of any sense of danger."

"You aren't the only one," I said, glancing at Carey. I had no idea what Carey made of their conversation, given that she could only hear Maura and not her brother, but her expression relaxed as she watched their banter.

"She knows you're a Reaper now," Carey said to Maura. "I wonder if she ran away because she's scared of you."

"Next time, I'll get her." Maura turned decisively away from the lake. "Let's move."

We hadn't taken three steps before Mattie's ghost appeared above the shore of the lake, bringing us to an immediate halt.

"You won't quit until you're dead, too, will you?" she said, addressing Maura. "I tried to warn you off, but you refused to listen. Then I hid, hoping you'd give up."

"But we didn't." Maura's gaze went from the ghost to the lake and back again. "The other spirit is the source of the rumours. Not you."

The ghost rolled her eyes. "However did you guess?"

"Was it her who threw me in the lake earlier?" I asked, already suspecting the answer.

"Does it matter?" Mattie said. "You already drew her attention, and now she'll be mad at all of you."

"Who is she?" Questions exploded in my mind. "Do you know one another? If you aren't the ghost from the stories, then why are you haunting the lake?"

"To warn people like you off." She gave me a derisive look. "Did you think I'd be *grateful* that you all paid a visit to my neglected grave and that you looked into my records? I guarantee that nobody cares that I'm gone."

"I'm sure that isn't true." The words came out automatically, but my mind was still reeling from the impact of knowing she *wasn't* the ghost we'd been searching for. "The other ghost—she's the one they call the Shadow on the Lake. How long has she been here?"

"Leave her alone," she growled. "Or she'll get you, along with everyone else you care about."

My heart dropped to my shoes. *The curse.* She couldn't be serious, could she?

"I very much doubt it," Maura said. "In fact, I'm coming back again later. This isn't over, not by a long shot."

"Maura." Not only was she a Reaper, but she could also leave Fairy Falls whenever she wanted to. The last thing we needed was for her to leave behind a permanent ghostly curse as a result of angering the Shadow on the Lake—though I'd partially been responsible too, because I hadn't stopped her.

Mattie didn't say another word. Instead, she vanished, leaving us on the lakeshore with even more questions than we'd started with.

———

"So what you're saying is not to go near the lake at midnight," Alissa remarked after I'd finished relating our hair-raising experience. Since she had an early-morning shift at the hospital, she'd been awake when I'd returned to the flat. I knew I should grab some sleep before work, but I'd run straight home after parting ways with Maura and the others, and now I was too wide awake to even think of going to sleep. Instead, I'd joined Alissa and the cats on the sofa in the living room.

"I should have taken my own advice." I stroked Sky, who grumbled in his sleep. "The Shadow on the Lake grabbed Carey as if she was solid and dragged her into the lake. I can see where the stories come from."

And the curse? A voice whispered in the back of my head. Was the Shadow on the Lake's next step to plague all of us with disaster? Maura seemed convinced being a Reaper made her immune, but the rest of us were all too human. And the ghost was no ordinary spirit—according to Maura, anyway.

"No kidding," said Alissa. "So the first ghost *wasn't* the Shadow on the Lake."

"Apparently not," I said. "Mattie did appear again,

though, to tell us we shouldn't have disturbed the Shadow on the Lake. Bit late for that, if you ask me."

"She knew?" Alissa asked. "I guess the local spirits must talk to each other, after all, and they do both live near the lake."

"Our new friend wasn't what I'd call talkative." I shivered. "Needless to say, we didn't find Mattie's missing body, but at this point, we know she isn't the one we're looking for."

"Then who is the other ghost? She must have had a real name at some point, right?"

"You'd think, but Maura claims she isn't a regular ghost. Whatever *that* means." I rubbed my arms, goose bumps prickling my skin. "Maura said she needs to do some digging into her memories of her Reaper apprenticeship to figure it out."

"You know, I'm starting to think going on a midnight ghost-hunting session with Maura wasn't the best of ideas, Blair."

"*I'm* starting to think that I got off lightly when the ghost only threw me into the lake without touching me."

Ghosts weren't supposed to be able to touch living people, though, let alone drag them around and throw them in lakes. Even Maura had said so, and she was the expert.

"Yeah, I agree," said Alissa. "Poor Mattie, getting blamed for this other ghost's mischief."

"More than mischief, if those two ghost hunters' deaths weren't accidental. What do you think of the curse now?"

Alissa pursed her lips. "I don't think it's a curse. I also don't see how the ghost can possibly have caused two people who were nowhere near the lake at the time to die in freak accidents. But I *do* think that we should leave any future ghostly meddling to Maura."

"What about Mattie, then?" I knew there was some kind of connection between the pair of them, but I couldn't for the life of me puzzle it out. "She said she stayed after death to warn people away from the Shadow on the Lake, but that implies the other spirit was there first."

Had the Shadow on the Lake killed *her*? Was that how she'd ended up haunting the lake?

"I don't know." Alissa yawned. "I need to get to work. I can ask about Fairfield House, the care home, if you like. I have a co-worker who grew up there. She might remember Mattie."

"Worth a shot." I assumed that it'd be common knowledge if Mattie had died as the result of a powerful ghost with the ability to drown people, but it didn't sound as if most people had known Mattie was dead at all. She'd been forgotten.

Alissa leaned across to stroke Roald and then rose to her feet. "See you later, okay? And please don't fight any more ghosts."

"Believe me, I don't plan to." Instead, I picked up my phone and messaged Nathan. Part of me wanted to warn him not to go near the lake when he was patrolling, but was I really that much of a wimp?

Mattie's warning flickered through my mind, reminding me that my fears were not unjustified. The ghost *had* grabbed Carey, and someone had tossed me into the lake as well. Even in the magical world, neither of those incidents was typical in the slightest.

My phone's vibration nearly made me jump out of my skin, but it was only Nathan calling me. *Get a grip, Blair.*

"Hey," I answered.

"Blair, what's going on?" he asked. "I'm on my way back from patrolling, but I thought you were staying at home with Alissa."

"She's gone to work, and I got attacked by a ghost."

"Seriously?" A pause. "Want to come over?"

"Yes, please." Next to me, Sky lifted his head and gave a disgruntled meow. "You've been lying there all day, Sky. It's not that big a deal to move to Nathan's."

Nathan stifled a laugh on the other end of the phone. "Come over and tell me everything."

10

Work the following morning was an ordeal. While I'd eventually managed to get some sleep thanks to Nathan's calm rationality in the face of my paranoia over the Shadow on the Lake maiming me in the middle of the night, I was not in the right headspace to focus on dealing with clients. I'd also utterly forgotten to do any preparation for my magic lesson afterwards, so I left the office at the end of the day with the grim expectation that I was bound to disappoint Rita again.

As I walked down the street, my phone buzzed in my pocket. I fished it out and found a couple of messages from Alissa. The first, sent several hours ago, gave me the address of Fairfield House, which I'd requested. The second message had been sent a few seconds ago, though, and it contained nothing more than the word "help."

My heart gave a jolt. I found my steps veering towards the high street, where I caught sight of a familiar hulking figure outside the hospital where Alissa worked. *Steve.*

Then I saw who he was talking to. Alissa wore her arm in a sling and another bandage on her leg, and the sight sent a quiver of alarm through me. When I reached the hospital, glass crunched beneath my feet, drawing my attention to a shattered upper-floor window. Two more gargoyles stood nearby.

"Alissa." I came to a breathless halt. "What happened to you? Are you okay?"

"Blair Wilkes," growled Steve. "How do you always manage to appear wherever there's trouble?"

"Because Alissa's my friend," I said. "Also, she sent me a message saying 'help.'"

"I did?" Her forehead scrunched up. "I don't remember that."

"This is ridiculous," Steve said, addressing Alissa. "You can't expect me to believe you were pushed out the window by an invisible man."

"A *what?*" I peered up at the shattered window. "Pushed out of the window? By whom?"

"That's the weird part," said Alissa. "It felt as if someone grabbed me, but there wasn't anyone there except for me."

"Too embarrassed to admit to tripping over your own feet?" Steve snorted.

"And you'd know about that?" I retaliated before I could think better of it. "Alissa isn't lying."

I didn't need my lie-sensing power to know that every word she said was the truth. Unfortunately, my comment drew Steve to project the full force of his angry gargoyle stare directly at me. "Don't you have somewhere else to be, Blair Wilkes?"

At that moment, one of Alissa's co-workers emerged

from the reception area. Lou, a friendly nurse with features that suggested Asian heritage, strode to Alissa's side. "Are the gargoyles giving you trouble?"

"They don't believe me," Alissa said. "Look, either someone used a spell to shove me out the window, or a hidden intruder pushed me. I didn't jump out myself."

An intruder. *A living one... or a dead one?* A voice whispered the question in the back of my mind before I could stifle it. Had the Shadow on the Lake somehow been responsible? It seemed absurd to think so, since Alissa hadn't been with us during last night's ill-advised jaunt... but I'd told her everything.

And Mattie... her warning had said the ghost wouldn't just target us but the people we cared about as well. I'd seen it for myself when the ghost had grabbed Carey and dragged her into the water.

"Are you sure it wasn't one of your patients who pushed you?" asked one of the other two gargoyles.

"I'd have seen if it was," she said firmly. "I'm telling the truth."

"We can't arrest someone invisible," Steve said.

"I'm not asking you to arrest anyone. I just want someone to search the premises for the intruder," she said. "Also, I think I lost my phone somewhere outside when I fell."

As the gargoyles argued with one another, I glimpsed Maura, Mart, and Carey approaching out of the corner of my eye. Sensing trouble, I went to waylay them before the police saw them coming.

"Maura." I caught up with her, barring her path down the street. "Your least favourite gargoyle is spoiling for a fight. I'd avoid this area until he's gone."

She peered past me at the hospital. "What's going on over there?"

"Alissa was attacked," I told her. "Something invisible dragged her out a window. Sound familiar?"

Her eyes rounded. "What? That's impossible."

"Alissa didn't see her attacker, but who else is disembodied and has a habit of grabbing people without warning?" I grimaced. "I didn't want to jump to conclusions, but I find it hard to believe this is a coincidence."

Carey went pale. "Alissa didn't come with us yesterday, though."

"I told her everything when I got back." My insides writhed with guilt. "Even if I hadn't, though… Mattie herself claimed that we'd brought danger upon everyone we care about by disturbing the Shadow on the Lake."

Maura pursed her lips. "If the ghost attacked her, she might still be in the area."

"Can't you look?" I asked.

"I can, but not in front of witnesses." She backed down the street, out of view of the gargoyles. "I'll check the afterworld, but there'd be more obvious signs if a ghost that dangerous was on the loose in public."

She was the expert, but if not the Shadow on the Lake, then I was at a loss to explain what had attacked Alissa. Or why.

I checked the time. I was already running late to my lesson. "I have a magic lesson I need to get to, but I'd stay away from the hospital until those gargoyles take off. Alissa is trying to convince them to search for the intruder."

"Good luck with that," muttered Maura. "That Steve

doesn't seem like he could find a visible intruder, let alone an invisible one."

Mart snickered. "Or even one wearing neon underpants with 'I am an Intruder' written on them."

"You aren't wrong," I acknowledged. "But our priority is the ghost, not Steve. Stay out of sight until the coast is clear."

"Right, fine." Maura rolled her eyes. "You know, I think we're in denial about this being resolved by tomorrow. After I look for the ghost, I'll call Allie and let her know we'll be staying a couple more days."

"Are you sure?" Carey asked. "I mean, are you actually going to tell her there might be a dangerous spirit hunting us?"

"Not just us." I glanced up at the hospital, my chest tightening. "The first person she targeted was my best friend, who never even set eyes on her. Where were you going, anyway? Not back to the lake?"

"Nah, to the library again," said Maura. "Out of the lack of any better options, because if the ghost is more than a regular spirit, we won't find that information in any library. The Reaper Council guards its knowledge closely."

"I'm starting to understand why you don't want them keeping an eye on you." I shook my head. "I thought you mentioned that you might have learned something during your apprenticeship that might help you identify that ghost."

"I didn't get a ton of experience out in the field, so I can't be certain of what it is." Frustration underlaid her tone. "It's definitely a spirit, though. I'll do some more digging after I call Allie."

"Try to stay out of trouble, won't you?" I checked the time, finding I'd gone from "running late" to "catastrophically late." "My lesson finishes in an hour, but I might have to stay longer to make up for lost time."

"Sure. You can find us then." Maura strode away while Mart rolled his eyes at her back.

"I think she's regretting sleeping through all her Reaper lessons," he told me. "Serve her right."

"You slept through all our lessons as well," Maura said over her shoulder at him.

He was a Reaper too. Being Maura's sibling, it made sense, and perhaps it accounted for his unusually strong presence as a ghost.

Yet I hadn't seen even Mart demonstrate enough strength to grab a living person and throw them around.

"See you soon." I broke into a run in the direction of the witches' headquarters, fighting the urge to skip my lesson and supervise Maura in case she antagonised Steve again while I was gone. Or drew the attention of another ghost. She made the term "one-woman force of chaos" look like an understatement, but there was no denying that she was also the person most likely to be able to deal with the Shadow on the Lake.

Needless to say, learning to recite the ingredients to a list of basic potions appealed as much as swimming in the lake currently did, but at least today's lesson was a theory one and not a practical one, so I had less chance of accidentally hexing Rebecca again.

"Goddess, Blair, your brain is like a cauldron full of holes," remarked Rita, waving my completed worksheet at me. "Honestly. You managed to give all the right answers but applied to the wrong questions."

"Oops." It wasn't my worst blunder, but Rebecca's perfect score hammered home my own ineptness.

"If you tried to brew this potion the way you wrote it out here, I'd have to evacuate the building before the floor collapsed," she added. "I know you have a lot on your mind, but you do need to focus on your studies if you ever hope to catch up to other witches your age."

Ouch. I debated telling her about Alissa's close call, but it would seem as if I was making excuses. Besides, what if Alissa had been targeted precisely because I'd confided in her? I didn't need the whole coven to end up suffering the wrath of the Shadow on the Lake too, so I held my tongue.

After the lesson ended, I left the witches' headquarters and headed back to the hospital in search of Alissa. She hadn't texted me, but she'd mentioned losing her phone in the aftermath of falling from the window. The police had departed, and someone had fixed the window, but there was no sign of Alissa inside the reception area.

Before I could walk in, I spied Maura and her companions lurking in an alleyway between the hospital and the neighbouring building.

"What are you doing here?" I veered towards them. "I thought you were going to the library."

"Allie said we can stay until the weekend," Carey said.

"Reluctantly," added Maura. "The police have gone, so I thought we could do some poking around."

"You can't just walk into the hospital and start hunting for ghosts in all the wards," I protested.

"She already did," Mart informed me. "Apparently, the ghost isn't there."

I groaned. "You're impossible."

"Nobody saw me, don't worry," said Maura. "Ghosts tend to haunt hospitals fairly frequently. I wonder if any of the other local spirits saw who attacked your friend."

"Go right ahead and ask them." If Maura wanted to draw the Shadow of the Lake's attention onto herself instead of the rest of us, then she was welcome to.

Darkness spread around Maura's outstretched hands, forming a wall of shadow in front of her. Addressing the darkness, she said, "Hey, there. Can I have a word?"

For a moment, nobody replied. Then a ghostly woman appeared from the gloom and shrieked, "It's a Reaper!"

"Relax, I'm not here for your soul," said Maura. "What's your name?"

"T-Tara." She trembled all over. "What do you want with me?"

"Not you," said Maura. "I'm looking for the other ghost."

"What other ghost?" The ghost looked at us with transparent, frightened eyes. "I don't know what you mean."

"The one who just attacked someone in the hospital earlier," I put in, discarding my resolution to let Maura handle this. After all, the other resident ghosts ought to have seen the intruder enter the building, unless none of them had been paying attention.

"I didn't see any ghosts attack anyone." Her voice trembled. "I didn't see anyone at all."

My lie-sensing power didn't work on spirits, but I couldn't figure out why she'd be less than truthful. The Shadow on the Lake might be as scary to ghosts as she was to humans, based on how Mattie had reacted. She'd even gone as far as to stick around the lake to warn us off, in fact.

"What about Mattie Lyons?" I asked the ghost. "Do you know her?"

She looked startled. "What? Why do you want to know?"

"You know her, don't you?" I pressed. "Did you know her before she died? Or after?"

"Why are you asking me all these questions when I'm not the ghost you're looking for?"

"You're not the ghost we're looking for?" Mart crowed in the background, laughing at his own *Star Wars* reference.

Ignoring him, Maura stepped in. "We're trying to find out how she died. It's important."

The ghost retreated into the shadows. "Leave me alone. Please."

She vanished, along with the darkness.

"Does that mean she knows Mattie?" The local ghosts might be familiar with one another, but that didn't necessarily mean they'd been acquainted with one another, let alone before their deaths. "Or the Shadow on the Lake? Was she lying, do you think?"

Maura glanced at me. "Might have been, but I don't see why she'd defend the Shadow on the Lake. Maybe it wasn't her who attacked your friend."

"It wasn't Mattie either," I said. "Besides, Alissa's description of the ghost's attack sounded exactly like the way Carey was dragged into the lake."

"Don't remind me." Carey shuddered. "Ah... didn't Alissa say she was going to find out more about Fairfield House?"

"She sent me the address, but I didn't have time to ask if she found out anything else." I turned towards the hospital. "I'll see if she's around, but I imagine she probably went home."

That, or she'd gone to the police station to continue with her futile quest to convince Steve to actually do his job for once.

"Looking for Alissa?" Lou asked as I walked into the reception area. "She left about fifteen minutes ago."

"Did she go to the police station?"

"No, she gave up on Steve." Her brow furrowed. "Who are those people you were talking to, anyway? They're not local."

"Tourists," I said vaguely, not wanting to give the Shadow on the Lake yet another target. "I was showing them around. Anyway, see you soon."

I left the hospital and pulled out my phone to get the address for Fairfield House. It wasn't far from here, but when Maura asked for the address, I hesitated. "Are you sure it won't draw out the Shadow on the Lake? I don't want it running amok around the local foster home as well."

"We don't need to reference the other ghost to find out what they remember about Mattie," she pointed out. "I won't say a word."

"All right."

I hoped it was worth the risk. Mattie was linked to the other ghost in some way, I was certain, and maybe helping her find peace was the key to getting rid of the Shadow on the Lake as well.

———

Fairfield House was marked by a cheery signpost decorated with unicorns and mermaids. It didn't look like an unpleasant place to grow up, judging by the sounds of children playing in the garden behind the building. Carey hovered farther back while Maura and I approached the red-painted door and knocked.

A middle-aged witch with wild black hair streaked with grey answered. "Hello, there. Can I help you?"

"Hey," I said. "This is kind of a weird question, but I wondered if I could ask about a former resident who used to live at Fairfield House. Did you ever know Mattie Lyons?"

Her expression clouded. "Yes, I did. It's a sad story, hers. She disappeared without a trace a few years ago, and nobody ever found her."

"Ah…" I glanced at Maura. "We found her ghost. Haunting the lake."

Tears brimmed in her eyes. "So she's dead. I always thought so, but…"

"But her body was never found," Maura finished.

"Yeah, I gathered. Also, she won't tell us how she died."

I gave her a warning look, but the woman had pulled out a handkerchief and was dabbing her eyes. "She left us several weeks before her disappearance."

"You mean she moved out?" I asked. "She was eighteen, right?"

"Barely seventeen," she croaked. "After dropping out of school, she fell in with a bad crowd and eventually ran away. We all tried to convince her to come back, but she was stubborn, and in the end… there wasn't anything we could do."

"I'm sorry," I said. "Erm, the police were looking for

her, right? Did they ever speak to this 'bad crowd' she was involved with?"

"Maybe. I don't know." She sniffed. "The police weren't bothered and quickly dropped the case after nothing showed up… but you mentioned that her ghost spoke to you?"

"She did." I scrambled for a way to explain how we'd found her without mentioning the Shadow on the Lake. "We heard a rumour about a ghost haunting the lake, and Mattie appeared when we went to look. She didn't mention how she died or if anyone else knew. Who were her friends?"

"I honestly don't know," she replied. "Other dropouts, kids who had nowhere to go. We do our best to take in anyone at risk, but some won't accept our help, and what can we do?"

"It's great. What you're doing, I mean." I felt my face heat up as I flailed in search of the right words. "I… I grew up in the foster system myself. In the normal world, I mean. I ended up turning out fine."

"That's good." Her eyes were watering again. "Very good. I… I'm glad to have some closure on what happened to Mattie, at least."

"I'm sorry I didn't have good news." My lie-sensing powers hadn't picked up on anything amiss, so she must have been telling the truth. "Bye."

Maura was already turning away from the house, her expression conflicted, and Carey looked a little tearful herself. Silence spread between us as we walked down the street—until Maura drew to a halt, her posture stiffening. "Who's there?"

I turned. A girl stood behind us, her messy hair in a

topknot and her jaw working as she chewed a piece of gum. I hadn't heard her following us, and neither, it seemed, had Maura.

"Heard you were asking about Mattie Lyons." She chewed on her gum. "Don't do that."

"Why not?" Maura frowned at her. "You knew her, did you?"

"You shouldn't ask so many questions." Her gaze slid between us, her eyes the murky colour of a neglected pond. "But if you really want to know the truth, then there's an old lady who lives by the lake who was still looking for Mattie after everyone else gave up on her. She lives at Number 7, Lakeside View."

My blood went cold. "Who is this woman? Why do you think she can help us?"

She turned her back and sprinted away, vanishing down a nearby side street as quickly as she'd arrived.

Maura stared after her. "Weird kid."

"Was *she* a ghost?" I rubbed my arms, shivers prickling up my spine. "She was kinda creepy."

"I've had enough of being screwed around." Maura turned away and took a pointed step forward. "Right, we're going to the lake."

"You're just going to follow her advice? Really?"

"Got any better ideas?" She quickened her pace with a determined expression.

"I can think of a few," Mart said. "If you fall into the lake yourself this time, it'll serve you right."

Since the Shadow on the Lake seemed intent on attacking everyone *except* Maura, then I doubted she'd be in any real danger. I, on the other hand, kept my Seven

Millimetre Boots turned on and my attention on my surroundings when we neared the lakeside once again.

Lakeside View wasn't much of a road, more of a half-hearted tangle of houses on the bank. A single cottage sat close enough to the water to be in danger of flooding, though the view from the windows might make up for it. The number 7 stood out crookedly on the door. This was the place.

An elderly witch with flyaway grey hair and a vague expression opened the door when Maura knocked. "Hello? Oh, I recognise you. You're the ones who created a disturbance by the lake the other night."

She'd seen us? *Did she see the ghost too?* "Erm, who are you?"

"The name's Evana Yarrow, and what you do at night is your own business," she went on. "Plenty of people like to go swimming with the merpeople. I won't judge you."

I glanced at Maura, who looked as bewildered as I did. "We're here to ask about Mattie Lyons, a girl who went missing a few years ago. Is it true that you were involved in the search for her after she disappeared near the lake?"

"What's this?" she asked. "Mattie Lyons?"

Maura stepped in. "Mattie used to live in foster care before she fell in with a bad crowd and then went missing. Her body was never found, but I was told that you kept searching after everyone else gave up."

"Who told you that?"

A weird girl who might have been a ghost.

"Never mind that," Maura answered. "You saw us the other night, did you? Were you looking out the window on the night Mattie went missing as well?"

The woman's expression turned peevish. "Who are you, dear? You're not local."

"We're here on holiday," Maura answered. "I am, anyway."

The woman squinted at me. "And you're Blair Wilkes."

"Yes." It shouldn't surprise me that she knew my name, given that half the town did, if not more. "Were you helping the police look for Mattie?"

"Did they send you?" She wrinkled her nose. "Steve?"

"No." I nodded to Maura. "We met Mattie's ghost by the lake the other day and found out that nobody knew she was dead."

"You met her ghost, did you?" Her gaze slid to Maura. "I can tell you're the troublesome sort. Making noise at night, frightening people, and generally being a nuisance. It's not appreciated. Some of us just want to be left alone."

Her change in tone startled me a little, but she was telling the truth as far as my lie-sensing power could work out.

"We just want to know—" Maura broke off when the woman retreated into the house, closing the door firmly behind her. "Thanks for the help."

I shook my head. "What was the point in that kid sending us here?"

"I don't know." Maura looked troubled. "She knows more than she told us, I'm certain, but I'm better at wringing answers from the dead than the living."

"Seems to me that none of the ghosts we meet are willing to talk either," I commented. "Anyway, if you want to poke her about the Shadow on the Lake, then feel free. I have to get home and see if Alissa is okay."

11

I let myself into the flat, where I found Alissa sitting on the sofa with her familiar curled up in her lap. Her arm was still in a sling, but her magical healing talents meant she'd be back on her feet in no time.

"Hey, Blair."

Next to her, Sky meowed a greeting. He'd moved back from Nathan's house during the day, apparently. I perched next to him. "Have you told Samuel yet?"

"No," she responded. "I never did find my phone. He'd want to come over anyway, and I'd rather wait until after he's done with work."

"He has his new fairy assistant to help out," I reminded her. "If she's back at the library, Maura is probably hassling him again too."

"Maura?" she echoed. "What's she done this time?"

"Where to start?" I told her everything, starting from our excursion to Fairfield House and ending at Maura's conversation with Evana Yarrow. I also added in my theory of who the real culprit was behind her injury.

"You think a *ghost* attacked me?" she asked sceptically.

"The Shadow on the Lake," I clarified. "She dragged Carey into the lake yesterday, and your description of the attack sounded exactly the same."

Her forehead crinkled. "So our Reaper visitor has set an aggressive ghost loose in town? Any more bad news I should know about?"

"She's also extended her stay until the weekend."

"Just what we need."

"I know, right?" I sighed. "To top it off, our investigation has hit a wall. The people at Fairfield House are grateful to have closure on Mattie's fate, but I can't figure out how she's linked to the Shadow on the Lake. Not at all."

The only people who might know the truth were dead, and the dead weren't talking at the moment. Not even to Maura.

A loud squeaking noise came from nearby, and the pixie who lived in our garden flitted through the living room, little wings beating frantically.

"What is it?" I asked him. "Please don't tell me the Elf King wants a piece of me too."

Without warning, Sky jolted upright. "*Miaow.*"

The sharp note in his voice had both of us on our feet, along with Roald the cat. An instant later, the window shattered as a large plank of wood came crashing through, striking the sofa in the exact spot where Alissa had been sitting a moment ago.

Roald yowled and ran into the bedroom, while Sky padded over to my side and tried to herd me out of the room. I stared at the plank of wood, disbelief coursing through me. It'd take a gargoyle's strength to pick up a piece of wood that large and throw it through the window.

A gargoyle… or a ghost.

———

Five minutes after escaping the flat, the pair of us stood at the police station, knowing that we'd be laughed out of the office and left to clear up the mess alone. I didn't need to be a Seer to predict how unamused Steve would be to see me again.

"Hey, Samuel's here," Alissa said, relief sweeping across her face. "Guess I should give him all the bad news at once, then."

At least with Samuel to back us up, the gargoyles might be more inclined to pay attention, but given their attitude earlier, maybe not.

"Alissa." Samuel glided to a halt in front of us, concern etched on his face. "I heard about an incident at the hospital earlier."

"I lost my phone earlier," she said. "But that's not the latest. Someone just threw a plank of wood through our living room window. Barely missed us."

As we'd discovered when we'd left the house, the plank of wood must have been ripped out of our own fence. It wasn't impossible for someone to have done it single-handedly if they'd used magic, but the lack of any foot-prints nearby said otherwise. Sky had opted to stay behind and guard the place. Maybe he was keeping an eye out for ghosts. Let's face it, even the Shadow on the Lake might think twice about crossing my cat.

"Who would do that?" Samuel's eyes narrowed. "Did you see anyone outside?"

"No... but I don't think it was a living person who threw it." I drew in a breath. "In fact, I think it was the Shadow on the Lake."

Samuel's gaze slid to me. "Explain."

He could have read the details from my thoughts, but I gave him a rundown of the events of the past day along with Alissa's input.

He muttered a curse under his breath when I'd finished. "That would explain why your Reaper friend was looking up books of dark magic in the library earlier."

"She wasn't, was she?" What was she up to this time? "What kind of dark magic exactly?"

"Rituals, among other things," he said. "If she is responsible for attacking you, however, then I will not allow her into my library again."

"She isn't... not directly," I clarified. "This Shadow on the Lake has been here for years. Most people have never heard of it."

"Until Maura poked it with a stick, effectively," added Alissa.

"She's not the first," I interjected before Samuel marched straight back to the library and unleashed his fangs on Maura. "I'm also pretty sure she's the only person in town who can get rid of it."

Before anyone could speak another word, Nathan hurried out of the police station. I'd texted him on the way, but I hadn't been able to cram all the details into a single text message.

"Blair, are you okay?"

"Thanks to my cat. And the pixie." Both of them had been quick on the mark, but since the pixie didn't speak English and Sky hadn't seen the attacker himself, neither would be able to confirm whether or not it had been the Shadow on the Lake. "We were going to go and explain to—"

"What is it this time?" Steve's voice boomed from inside the police station. "Not you again, Blair Wilkes."

Here we go. Resigned to another face-off, I walked through the automatic doors with Nathan, Alissa, and Samuel.

"Someone threw a plank of wood through our window," Alissa told the unimpressed gargoyle. "Possibly the same someone who attacked me at the hospital earlier."

"Your invisible assailant." Derisiveness dripped from his words. "You can't report a ghost. If you're telling the truth, that is, which I very much doubt."

"You can see the plank of wood for yourself if you come to our house," I said. "It's huge. If a living person did it, they either used magic or have unnatural strength. Like a…. er, werewolf." Using the gargoyle comparison would not help the situation.

He grunted. "If you didn't see your attacker, then what do you want me to do? Arrest the invisible man?"

"Do you want me to bring my grandmother to convince you to help us?" Alissa enquired. "Can you at least have a look around our garden to confirm nobody broke in?"

Steve glowered at her. "I will send a team to assess the damage after you've filed a report."

"Good." Samuel's fangs gleamed as he looked up at the

gargoyle shifter. "I expect you to treat this situation as seriously as is merited."

"I'll have a look around the house," Nathan offered. "To make sure the attacker isn't in the area."

If it is, most of us won't be able to actually see it. "I'll go with you after we're done with the report."

"I'll handle the report myself," Alissa said. "I'm not going home until that ghost is definitely gone."

Nathan and I left the police station behind, at which point I said, "I think it might take Maura's help to be certain there aren't any ghosts around. Neither of us can see into the afterworld."

"Isn't she the reason you were attacked in the first place?"

"Kind of." I sighed. "Since our encounter with that ghost last night, someone has tried to throw Alissa out of a window and almost crushed the pair of us to death. I'm not sure which of us was the target, frankly."

"Anyone with magic could have done the same," Nathan said. "It's not that I don't believe you, Blair, but if it *is* a ghost, then there's nothing the police will be able to do to help. Nobody on the team can see ghosts."

"Typical," I muttered. "What're the odds that the same monster attacking us is also responsible for those two ghost hunters' deaths too?"

"Ghost hunters?" His brow furrowed. "Who?"

"The guy who initially wrote the article that drew Maura's attention to the lake died in a car crash not long ago," I explained. "Also, the man who dropped dead while I was with my parents at the café turned out to be a ghost hunter as well as a wizard. After you told me about him, I searched his name on the Wizarding Web."

He blinked. "You think this ghost was responsible for his death?"

"He was looking for the Shadow on the Lake, same as Maura," I explained. "Mattie's ghost explicitly told us that the reason she was haunting the lake was to warn people off. She claimed that if we didn't, the Shadow on the Lake would target everyone we cared about…"

"You can't tell if ghosts are telling the truth, though, can you?" He slowed his pace when we neared the house. "They can lie."

"I know they can, but *someone* did this." I indicated the damaged window ahead of us. "Someone who has a grudge."

Our upstairs neighbour, Nina, approached us from the garden. "What's going on out here? I heard the noise from upstairs."

"We're not sure, but the police are on their way."

I didn't want to freak out Nina by detailing the possible situation with the Shadow on the Lake, especially given that Alissa had been targeted without setting eyes on the creature herself. Nathan and I searched the garden, but no traces of the attacker—if any had ever existed—had been left behind.

Halfway through our search, Steve's team swooped in and pounced on Nina, sensing an easy target. While I was insisting that she couldn't possibly have attacked us from *inside* the building, Samuel appeared in a blur, his gaze fixed on the window.

"Did you leave Alissa at the police station?" I asked him.

"She insisted on staying to give her statement and fill out the report." He examined the shattered glass, ignoring the gargoyles lumbering around in the background. "Does your Reaper friend know your wayward ghost seems to have committed property damage?"

My heart missed a beat. "You know she's a Reaper?"

"Of course I do." His mouth turned down at the corners, displaying his fangs. "I couldn't read her mind when she came in, and there were only a handful of reasons that would be the case. I knew she wasn't a vampire or fairy, so there was one remaining conclusion to reach."

"Is she still in the library?"

"No, she left before I did." He stalked towards the broken fence on the lawn. "But if she is responsible for this, then I believe she ought to pay for the damage."

"She couldn't have known this was coming." I turned to Nathan in the hopes that he'd back me up, but he wasn't fond of Maura either. "She's the expert on ghosts. I think we should let her know."

Nathan looked unimpressed. "To be quite honest, I don't entirely trust her not to make the situation worse."

Part of me agreed, but it wasn't Maura who'd set the ghost loose to begin with, and while Samuel's ire was justified, driving her out of town would only hurt all of us.

"Come on." I squeezed Nathan's hand. "We'll walk to the lake. I bet she's over there."

Nathan reluctantly turned away from the house. "Unfortunately, I can't see ghosts. Give me a living problem to deal with and I can do it, no problem. But this..."

"Believe me, being able to see ghosts doesn't make someone any more adept at figuring them out." I walked alongside him out of the garden and down the road. "Even vampires wouldn't be able to sink their fangs into a ghost."

"No doubt that's why Samuel would rather have a living target," he said in a low voice. "Especially one who might be partly responsible for this."

"Vampires don't like Reapers anyway," I told him. "I might not agree with everything Maura did, but she didn't intend any of this to happen, and I think she can help us figure out the cause."

"I suppose." He sounded doubtful, but he didn't turn back.

We walked to the lakeside, where I spotted Maura and the others standing on the shore. I didn't see any nearby ghosts, but I kept a wary eye on the water's surface as I approached them.

"Blair," she said. "Back already?"

"The Shadow on the Lake just threw a plank of wood through my window and nearly crushed Alissa and me."

Carey's jaw dropped. "What?"

Maura blinked. "That's new. Are you sure it was her?"

"No, but this is twice Alissa has been attacked in the space of a day, and I want answers." I indicated Nathan. "This is Nathan, my boyfriend and head of the town's security team. The police are at the house, but we'd greatly appreciate it if you had a look around the property to see if anything is hiding in the afterworld."

Her brow arched. "While the police are there? Really?"

"Well… maybe keep your distance from them. And from Samuel too." I scanned the lake. "What are you doing? Not pestering Mattie again?"

Maura shrugged. "She's the one ghost who had anything vaguely useful to say."

"She also warned us to leave the lake alone," I said. "Also, Samuel told me you were researching dark magic at the library."

"Ritual magic," she corrected. "Odds are, that's how this ghost ended up bound to the lake. Most strong spirits are the result of a ritual."

"A ritual?" I echoed. "You think that's why she's powerful enough to cause people to run into misfortune? Like those ghost hunters?"

"I can't say for certain," she said. "Not without talking to someone with direct experience."

"What, talking to the ghost hunters?" *Wait a moment.* "The guy who dropped dead last weekend… do you think *his* ghost might still be around?"

"Last weekend?" She wore a thoughtful expression. "Might be. Where'd he die?"

"On Saturday, in Sloan," I replied. "It's a normal town, not too far away from here. From what I saw, he dropped dead of no apparent cause."

An interested gleam appeared in her eyes. "You know, I wouldn't mind getting his perspective. I'll have a look around your house first and see if the perpetrator's still there."

"You really think a ghost did that much damage?" Nathan studied her, his brow furrowed. "Do you make a habit of unleashing dangerous spirits?"

"Hey, don't look at me," Maura said. "The ghost hunter's the one who annoyed the Shadow on the Lake before I got here. Not to mention the guy who wrote the first article and started the whole thing to begin with."

"They weren't local to Fairy Falls." A muscle flickered in Nathan's jaw. "And they sought out the trouble themselves. Blair didn't."

Oh boy. Maura's expression signalled a challenge, and if he and Maura went head to head, then I wasn't sure who'd come off worse.

"I kind of did," I said. "Come on, let's go back to the house and do some ghost hunting. Also, Maura, I'd avoid Samuel. He worked out you were connected to Alissa being targeted twice in a day."

"Right." She turned her back on the lake and walked behind Nathan and me. After a long pause, she added, "I didn't mean for this to happen, you know. It shouldn't be possible for a creature that powerful to lurk around for years without being detected. It took me off guard."

"Wow, you actually admitted to making a mistake?" Mart drifted next to her, unseen by anyone except for Maura and me.

We retraced our steps to the house and stopped at a safe enough distance away so as not to be spotted by the police while Maura searched for any ghostly trespassers. Nathan's brows shot up when darkness spread around her hands and she looked into the afterworld.

A moment later, she dropped her arms. "Nothing there."

"Seriously?" I said.

"I've never seen anyone look so disappointed to learn their house is *not* haunted."

Mart hooted with laughter.

I frowned at him. "It'd be easier if the ghost were here, that's all."

"There's still that ghost hunter," said Maura. "How far a walk is Sloan from here?"

"Long enough that it'll be dark by the time you get back. You don't want to go now, do you?"

"I have a broom," she said. "The longer we wait, the more likely it is that his ghost will move on."

I turned to Nathan. "I'll go with her."

"No." He shook his head firmly. "Not alone."

"I need you to argue my case with Steve." It might be too late for me to keep the ghost away from Alissa, but I refused to let her target Nathan as well. "You know he'll drop it if someone doesn't put pressure on him. Alissa and Samuel will try, but they'll appreciate you backing them up."

His expression turned conflicted. "If you're sure, but I don't like this."

"I am." Leaving him behind stung, but if I'd brought the ghost on Alissa's tail, then I could at least spare Nathan the same fate.

A loud "miaow" sounded, and a moment later, Sky padded towards me and halted at my feet.

"Hey." I looked down at him, wondering if he'd been following me the whole time. "What is it?"

"I think he's volunteering to go with you," Nathan said. "Good idea. I'd feel a lot more secure if you took him along."

"Well… all right."

Sky sprang into my arms and meowed at a bemused Maura. "Is he your familiar?"

"Yeah, this is Sky." He wasn't a typical familiar, but he'd defend me without hesitation. "I guess Reapers don't generally have familiars?"

"Having my brother's ghost attached to me is more than an effective enough substitute, to be honest."

"I'm far better than a familiar, since I can talk," Mart announced.

"Miaow," said Sky.

"Sky has his own set of skills." Like turning into a giant monster when I was under threat, for instance. With him at my side, I felt less like we were making a huge mistake in leaving Fairy Falls, even temporarily.

If the Shadow on the Lake had us on her hit list, though, then we could do worse than to talk to one of her past victims.

12

After parting ways with Nathan at the border of Fairy Falls, I crossed the fields and hills to the nearby town of Sloan. Maura and Carey flew on their broomsticks, while I brought out my fairy wings with a snap of my fingers and let Sky perch on my shoulder. He seemed to enjoy the ride over the hillside, which was some compensation for waking him from his nap, I supposed. No hikers were wandering the hills at seven in the evening on a weekday, and we reached our destination without having to take a detour to avoid curious normals.

I swooped to a halt next to Maura, who eyed my shoulders. "What's with the...?"

"Wings?" I should have known *that* would bring up a new set of questions, but I'd been too impatient to use my boots, and I was not a fan of broomsticks. "I'm half fairy, half witch."

"Fair enough." She and Carey dismounted their broomsticks, and Maura made them disappear with a wave of her wand, seemingly unperturbed by my revelation. It was no weirder than a Reaper witch, after all. "I'll search for that ghost. Where are we least likely to be spotted by normals?"

"Out here, provided there aren't any hikers around." An evening on a weekday was hardly the ideal time for a hike, so we were safe in that regard, but I still kept an eye out for any bystanders as we walked into the outskirts of Sloan. "I don't know how close you have to be to the place where the person died to contact their ghost, but he dropped dead at a public shopping centre."

"You can't use your power there, Maura," Carey told her. "Not in front of witnesses."

"I wasn't planning to," she responded. "If the ghost is around, I should theoretically be able to reach him even from out here. What's his name again?"

"Leroy Quint."

"Right." She walked a short distance before coming to a halt and holding out her hands. Shadows crept in around her, masking the area in front of her from sight. "Leroy Quint?"

For a while, no response came from the gloom. Then Maura took a startled step back as a ghost floated out of the shadows. It was definitely the same man who'd dropped dead outside the café, except he was now transparent and glowing faintly around the edges. Instead of looking scared to see a Reaper, his expression showed outright annoyance.

"You." Leroy Quint pointed at me. "I know you. I've seen you before."

"Excuse me?" Our eyes had locked briefly through the

café window, yes, but my dad and I had been fully glamoured. "You mean at the café? Before you…"

"Died." His gaze shifted to Maura next. "You're a Reaper. Are you here to help me move on?"

"If you need a hand, then sure," said Maura. "But I'd like to ask you some questions first."

"That's not what Reapers do." His gaze darted between us. "Where's your scythe? Who are these people?"

I assumed he meant Carey and me… and Sky, who'd jumped off my shoulder to land at my feet.

"I said I was going to ask *you* questions, not the other way around." Maura pushed on. "How did you die?"

"You're not with the Reaper Council. They don't ask questions."

"Just our luck to get a pedant," Maura muttered. "Look, be grateful I showed up at all. Why did you stick around this long after your death?"

"I don't have to talk to you." The ghost turned his back pointedly.

Maura held out a hand and touched his arm, and he recoiled. "I might not be an official one, but I have all the skills of a Reaper and a willingness to use them. Tell me what you know."

The ghost scowled at her over his shoulder. "You're not going to quit, are you?"

"Nope," she said. "Mostly because we think the creature that killed you is after us too."

"You're joking." Incredulity rippled across his features. "Don't tell me you went to that lake. You didn't, did you?"

Dread gripped me. So it was true. The ghost *had* killed him… and he thought we'd be next.

"Okay, we won't tell you." Mart flew up to hover

alongside his sister. "The Shadow on the Lake, right? The ghost that only comes out at midnight?"

"Stay away from that lake," Leroy warned. "I'm not the first that spirit has killed, and I won't be the last."

"Too late, unfortunately," I said. "How'd she kill you? I didn't see any ghosts near you when you died."

He flinched. "I don't know."

Maura arched a brow. "You don't?"

"No. One second I was walking around; the next, I was... here." He gestured at the shadows which outlined his transparent figure. "I wasn't exactly in a state of mind to question anyone about how I got here. I was too busy watching them carry my body away... and you." He addressed me. "You were there."

"Yes, but I didn't realise your ghost stayed behind." I'd been more concerned with getting my foster parents out of the way in case his death had turned out to have a magical cause.

"There's usually a lag," Maura said. "Between your death and reappearance."

I didn't hear the ghost's reply. A shiver of dread raced down my spine as I recalled my conversation with Mr Wilkes on the phone, in which he'd referred to all the misfortune he'd run into this week.

No... the Shadow on the Lake couldn't be targeting my foster parents. They didn't live anywhere near the lake. I hadn't told them a thing...

"Did you actually see the Shadow on the Lake?" Maura asked the ghost. "In the flesh... I mean, spirit?"

He shuddered. "Yes, and it's not a sight I'll forget in a hurry. I thought I could get some video footage of her from a distance, but she still saw right into my hiding place."

"You have video footage?" Maura asked. "Did you have your camera with you when you died?"

"No, I dropped it in the bushes somewhere near the lake when the ghost *grabbed* me." He gave another violent shudder. "I managed to break free of her hold, by some miracle, and ran like hell. I hid in a ditch for the rest of the night and then went to the nearest safe haven. Or I thought so."

"But she got you," Maura concluded. "Did you stop by in Fairy Falls at any point?"

"No, I didn't," he said. "Why?"

"A local ghost warned us off looking for her," I explained, assuming Maura wanted to know if he'd seen Mattie Lyons too. "I live in Fairy Falls myself, and since we saw the Shadow on the Lake, we've had two narrow escapes. A friend of mine was injured in the first one, and she never actually saw the ghost herself. Do you know if she typically goes after her victims' friends or...?" I couldn't say the word *family*. My insides felt full of writhing snakes.

"How should I know?" he asked. "I can hardly call my family when I'm dead."

My breath caught. My foster parents didn't even know the magical world existed, but they'd seen the man's death for themselves, even if they hadn't known the cause.

"What is it?" Maura caught my gaze. "You think the ghost might have targeted someone else?"

"My foster parents," I whispered. "They're normals, and they've been talking about weird accidents happening to them all week. Like what happened to Alissa but not as serious."

Yet, whispered a voice in my head.

"You think it's her?"

"I don't know, but it's not like they can see her." Nobody else living in their normal community would see the threat either. "They're completely unprepared for this."

"Tricky." Maura pursed her lips. "You might want to call them. I don't want anyone else getting hurt if I can help it—and the Shadow on the Lake can't be in more than one place at once—but if it puts your mind at ease, then I'd do it."

"All right." Hands shaking, I retrieved my phone from my pocket and left the others with the ghost before calling my foster parents.

"Hello?" Mr Wilkes's familiar voice answered. "Blair?"

"Hey," I said, a little breathless, my heart lurching against my rib cage. "Are you doing okay?"

"Never better." His tone sounded normal. Not at all as if he was being threatened by a ghost… and I intended to keep it that way. "You?"

"Yes—no. I mean, I don't know. There's a lot going on." I tried to slow my breathing to calm my racing thoughts. "Have you fixed your car? No more trouble?"

"No. Is work stressing you out?

He's okay. Relief flooded me, tempered by the grim knowledge that there was no guarantee that simply speaking to him wouldn't paint another target on his head. "A bit. Erm, sorry, gotta go. Alissa has something she needs my help with."

I hoped he didn't hear the worry in my voice, but there was no help for it. I didn't want to bring my foster parents into the magical world under circumstances as jarring as their previous encounter with the fairies, but if I had to use magic to keep them safe, I'd do it.

I ended the call and returned to Maura's side, only to find that Leroy Quint was no longer there. "Where's the ghost?"

"I banished him, like I promised," Maura said. "He didn't have anything else to tell us. Are your parents okay?"

"Yeah, but there's no guarantee the Shadow on the Lake will leave them alone if we keep antagonising her," I said. "She doesn't seem to care whether the people she targets are in the normal world when she strikes them down. Look at Leroy Quint."

"Point taken," said Maura, "but he might have got video footage of the ghost before he died. On our way back to Fairy Falls, I'll see if I can find that camera of his."

"Now you want to steal from a dead man?" I asked incredulously. "It's rained more than once since last weekend. If he dropped his camera in the bushes, it'll be of no use even if someone hasn't nicked it."

"It's worth seeing if he got any footage of our grumpy ghost." She turned back to face the rolling hills. "He doesn't remember the details of his death, so I still don't know *how* the Shadow on the Lake killed him. There are certainly spells or nasty curses that can make someone drop dead, but ghosts don't have access to that kind of magic."

"Even ghosts who were summoned using illegal ritual magic?" I asked.

"As far as I'm aware—yes." She pulled out her wand and conjured her broomstick, and Carey did the same.

I hesitated for a moment, reluctant to leave my foster

parents to potentially face the ghost's wrath. Yet they'd be better off staying far away from me until the threat was dealt with, and the quickest way to ensure their safety was to get rid of that ghost.

I snapped my fingers and brought out my wings. "Let's go back, Sky."

———

By the time I met Nathan at the border of Fairy Falls, it was almost fully dark, the sun having slipped away beyond the horizon. Sky hopped off my shoulder when I slowed down, landing at my feet.

Nathan strode up to greet me with a brief kiss. "How'd it go?"

"We did speak to the ghost." I gestured at the darkening field behind me. "Maura went to look for his camera to see if he got footage of the Shadow on the Lake before he died. He dropped it in the bushes somewhere."

Nathan's brows shot up. "The Shadow on the Lake killed him?"

"Looks that way." Worry crawled up my throat. "And— I'm concerned that my foster parents will be targeted. Some weird things happened to them earlier this week. Car breaking down, roof tiles falling, that type of thing. And Alissa has already been targeted."

"Blair." He drew me into an embrace. "It'll be okay."

I blinked hard, unexpected tears stinging my eyes. "I wish I'd never gone with them in the first place, but it's too late now. How are we supposed to fight something that can barely be seen and that can kill people without being anywhere near them?"

Nathan held me against him, his steady presence soothing my nerves. "Your Reaper friend thinks the ghost hunter has video footage?"

"Even if his camera survived getting soaked in the rain for days, it won't show us anything we haven't already seen when we saw the Shadow on the Lake ourselves," I mumbled against his chest. "Maura is as clueless as the rest of us, but she thinks the Shadow on the Lake might be the result of some kind of dark-magic ritual."

"And she still wants to hunt her down?"

"So do I." If not for myself then for Alissa's and my foster parents' sakes. Not to mention everyone else I cared about, like Nathan and—wait. "I wonder if my dad has seen anything. I don't think most fairies can see ghosts, but they still see things the rest of us don't."

"True," said Nathan. "We can pay him a visit if it makes you feel better."

"Might as well." If nothing else, my dad deserved to know that he might be a potential target too. Unlike my foster parents, he knew all too well how deadly the magical world could be.

Nathan and I walked up the path alongside the lake until we reached the nearest entrance into the forest and went in search of the fairies' part of town. Even the Shadow on the Lake would have a hard time finding her way to the fairies' home, which existed inside a kind of bubble that was invisible to anyone who couldn't see through glamour. That didn't mean regular people couldn't find their way in, though, and since Nathan had walked this route with me before, he soon tracked down the semitransparent path, which lay atop the forest as if it had grown out of the trees.

When we stepped onto the path, it shimmered underfoot. The forest rippled around us until the night-shrouded trees were replaced by bright paths that wound between clearings filled with tranquil cottages and patches of colourful flowers.

"I'll wait here." Nathan halted. "The other fairies get uneasy around me. I can tell."

"They shouldn't." Some of the fairies had had bad experiences with paranormal hunters, and while Nathan wasn't an active one anymore, the fear remained, especially since some of them didn't have a good relationship with Steve either. Pity the ghosts hadn't decided to haunt *him.*

"Miaow." Sky trotted up the path to join me.

"I think he came to visit his friends," said Nathan. "I'll wait for you here, okay?"

"All right."

With Sky at my side, I walked the rest of the way to the clearing where my dad's house stood. Like the other fairies, he lived in a neat cottage nestled between tall trees and surrounded by bright patches of wildflowers. Glamour shone from its walls, and the cheery red door opened before I could knock.

"Blair." He smiled at me. "It's great to see you."

"Hey, Dad." I glanced over my shoulder to make sure nobody was listening in. "Weird question. Has anyone seen any ghosts lately?"

"Ghosts?" he echoed. "No, but I'm not sure anyone in here *can* see them. Why?"

"There's a particularly nasty ghost after me, and I think you might be in danger."

"Come in." He took a step back, allowing me to enter the house. "Tell me about it."

The inside of his house was as pleasant as the exterior, with simple wooden furniture and bright paintings hanging on the walls. My dad favoured a minimalist approach, like me, but the place was cosy and warm.

I sat in one of the round armchairs, and the whole story came pouring out of me as my dad listened patiently. Sky, meanwhile, curled up on the thick rug at my feet and went to sleep. *Did he just come here to find somewhere else to take a nap?*

"I've never met a Reaper before," Dad remarked when I'd finished.

"Neither had I, until Maura. In fact, I'd never even heard of them." I glanced down at my sleeping cat. "She's half Reaper, half witch, and doesn't care much for rules. She poked that ghost, and now she's mad at us, and there's a risk that she might go after our friends and loved ones unless we can calm her down."

His brow furrowed. "I haven't heard of any ghostly activity in the area, but I've been busy helping new fairies move to town. Oh, I heard you got Ani a new position at the library. She's very grateful."

"Ah—that's good. I should have asked her how it went." At least one thing had gone right this week. "It's been a long day. Alissa's been attacked twice, but the ghost might have been aiming for me the second time around. She threw a plank of wood through our living room window."

He sucked in a breath. "Do you want to spend the night here instead?"

"I appreciate the offer, but I don't think this is going to stop until we get rid of the ghost altogether," I admitted.

"Even Maura doesn't know how she got so powerful, but she seems to think she can get rid of her anyway. And I don't know what else to do."

"Where is Alissa now?"

"At home… well, she might still be giving her statement at the police station," I said. "Steve is being as unhelpful as ever, but he can't see ghosts, let alone arrest them."

"Tricky," he said. "I can come and help out if you need me to."

"Nathan is waiting for me," I said, "and Maura went to find the camera one of the ghost's victims dropped to see if he got any decent footage. I'm not sure what more we can do."

"If the ghost intends to target the citizens of the town, then I'll do my best to help protect them." Dad looked down at Sky. "I'll come with you. Your cat won't mind if he wakes up and finds us gone?"

"Sky does whatever he wants." He'd show up if I needed him—of that I was certain. "We should go and find Nathan."

After my dad had locked up the house, we made for the path out of the fairies' part of the forest. Nathan wasn't waiting where I'd left him, but I continued to walk, wondering if he'd had to retreat to avoid drawing the fairies' attention. I didn't blame some of them for fearing the hunters, but I wished they'd give Nathan a chance.

Abruptly, the clearing vanished, the brightness replaced by the dark shadows of the regular forest—and a shout came from somewhere nearby.

Nathan.

13

I ran in the direction of Nathan's shout, veering around the trees, my dad fast on my heels. When we emerged onto the path, I spotted Nathan struggling to restrain a small figure. For a moment, I thought it was one of the elves. Then I saw her face and recognised the teenage witch we'd run into at Fairfield House. At least I now knew she wasn't a ghost if the way she was struggling against Nathan's grip was any indication.

"You again?" I strode over to her. "What are you doing?"

Nathan held her firmly but gently. "She was trying to get into the fairies' part of the forest."

Her gaze fixed on me, and she stopped struggling for a brief moment, but she didn't say a word.

"Why?" I frowned. "Was she looking for me?"

"You know one another?"

"I saw her by Fairfield House earlier," I explained. Addressing the girl, I asked, "What are you doing in here?"

"Casting a spell," Nathan answered for her. "Not a pleasant one either. Where'd you learn that?"

"None of your business," the girl spat. "Let me go."

"A spell?" I'd thought there was something odd about her, and now my suspicions had grown. "Want to come and tell Steve instead of us?"

Nathan didn't look too thrilled at my suggestion, but I was all too happy to make this Steve's problem instead of ours. We didn't need to deal with a teenage intruder on top of a ghost.

"You're coming with me." He carried the wriggling teenager down the winding path and out of the forest, at which point she stopped fighting and let herself be carried the rest of the way to the police station.

My dad and I walked behind Nathan, but neither of us followed him through the automatic doors when he carried his reluctant passenger inside.

"I wonder what she was doing there," I whispered to my dad. "I don't know if Steve will be able to pry answers from her, but using magic right next to the fairies' part of town is a great way to get turned into a toadstool."

I had my suspicions about her reasons for being in the forest, but a quick look through the automatic doors told me that Alissa didn't appear to be in the police station any longer, unless she'd gone into one of the smaller questioning rooms.

"Want to go in?" Dad asked.

"Not yet," I replied. "I'll go back home and find Alissa. I think she'll want to know what we found out."

My dad kept pace with me while I walked down the darkened streets and back to the house. The first thing I noticed was that someone had removed the broken glass and boarded up the shattered window, but the gargoyles were no longer there. Neither was Alissa that I could see. Dad waited outside while I unlocked the door and peered into the flat, but she was nowhere to be seen.

"She isn't there?" Dad asked when I returned to his side.

"She wasn't in the police station, either, but I suppose she might have gone home with Samuel." I wasn't clear on where he lived—in the library for all I knew—which I supposed was marginally safer than our flat was at the present time. All the same, worry fluttered in my chest, especially when I remembered she didn't have her phone.

Turning away from the house, we retraced our steps to the police station. As we reached the high street, Maura, Mart, and Carey approached from the opposite direction. I stifled a groan. "Hang on. I'll make sure Steve doesn't spot them."

Leaving my dad to wait outside the police station, I ran over to meet them. Without giving me the chance to speak first, Maura triumphantly held up a rather muddy camera. "Found it. And get this—it still works."

"You weren't going to give it to the police, were you?"

"I was looking for you. I figured you'd be here."

"You guessed right." I sucked in a breath. "Here's a new complication. We found someone trying to break into the fairies' territory in the forest. That creepy kid who spoke to us earlier was casting a spell until Nathan caught her."

"Weird." She held up the camera. "Want to see what Leroy Quint saw?"

"Not particularly." The ghost hunter's footage hardly mattered at this point anyway, but Maura plainly wasn't paying attention to anyone else. When she turned on the camera, I leaned over her shoulder.

The screen turned on, and the image of the lake flickered into view, its dark expanse visible despite the trees shadowing the edges of the screen. The trees explained how the camera had escaped the worst of the rain damage, but all questions fled my mind when something flickered on the lake's surface.

An instant later, the camera went spinning downward into the mud, landing on its side. Maura tilted the camera so we could watch, and the screen showed the ghost hunter's body flying towards the water, dragged by an invisible force.

My heart beat faster as I watched the ghost hunter struggle. He fought the ghost's grip, reaching into his pocket and pulling out what appeared to be a wand. A flash of light blurred the screen, followed by another. When the view came back into focus, the ghost hunter had seized his chance to run, feet slipping in the mud, until he disappeared from sight.

The camera remained on its side, showing the blurred edge of the lake. For a long, tense few seconds, nothing happened. The ghost hunter had gone, and I assumed that it'd kept filming until the camera had run out of battery life or storage space. Maura didn't turn it off, however, and eventually, movement stirred by the lake again. This time, a figure stepped out of the shadows and crossed the camera's vision, following the ghost hunter.

"That doesn't look like the ghost," I commented. "It's a living person."

"She has a point," Carey ventured. "Right, Maura?"

"Exactly," Maura muttered. "I wonder who it is. I bet

there's more footage on here, since it would have kept filming until the battery ran out."

"We don't have time to watch the whole thing." I looked up at the police station's doors. "I want to hear what that kid has to say."

"What *was* she doing?" asked Carey.

"I think she was trying to cast a spell on the fairies, too, but Nathan caught her at it," I explained. "My dad lives in that part of the forest. I went to check up on him in case the so-called curse targeted that side of my family as well, and we ran into her on our way back."

A thoughtful expression crossed Maura's face. "I wonder…"

"Something's fishy," I said. "If our teenage witch starts talking, she might give us some insight into what's really going on, but I bet Steve will kick up a fuss if he sees us hanging around while he questions her."

When I peered through the doors, I glimpsed her in the police station's entryway, no longer restrained. She was also surrounded by hulking gargoyles as well as Nathan, but her defensive posture showed no traces of fear.

My phone buzzed in my pocket, and my adrenaline spiked when I saw the message from Alissa: *Help. The Shadow on the Lake has me.*

My head snapped up. "They have Alissa."

"Who?" Carey asked. "Not the ghost?"

"I—don't know. She lost her phone earlier, and I don't know if she got it back, but ghosts can't usually send messages anyway."

"Hey!" Mart said indignantly. "Some of us can."

"No." Maura shook her head. "No, if someone is messaging you, it isn't a ghost."

"I figured." My heartbeat quickened. "But they have her phone, if not Alissa herself. Maybe I can call her and use the ringtone to track down where they are."

"Blair." My dad approached me. "What is it?"

"Alissa is messaging me, saying the Shadow on the Lake has taken her," I said. "I don't know if it's really her, but—did anyone see her leave the police station?"

The doors slid open, and Clare, the receptionist, shot me a glare when I walked in. "Wait outside. There's too many people already in here."

"Where's Alissa?" I asked. "Did she go home? Was Samuel with her?"

"I didn't ask."

"Blair." Nathan made his way over to me. "Everything okay?"

"Did you see where Alissa went?"

"Home, I assume."

"She isn't there, and neither is Samuel," I replied. "I just got this creepy message that seems to be from her."

I showed him, and his brows shot up. "Are you sure it's really her?"

"If it isn't, someone has her phone, and they're trying to get at me." I wouldn't know for sure until I found them, and did I really want to risk Alissa's safety? I returned my phone to my pocket, hands trembling. Despite my rattled nerves, however, I now knew beyond a shadow of a doubt that it wasn't a ghost we were dealing with at all.

I looked for the teenage witch and saw her sullenly staring down three gargoyles. When she saw me looking, she winked.

"Has she said anything yet?" I whispered to Nathan. "I think she's involved with the people who took Alissa. She's playing with us somehow."

"She hasn't," he said. "She did admit she's a resident at Fairfield House. Steve has called them to come and collect her, since she's a minor, but that spell she tried to use… I didn't recognise it, but I was taught to know dark magic by sight when I worked for the hunters."

My stomach lurched. "Maura has video footage of Leroy Quint, the ghost hunter, from the lake. When he ran away from the ghost, someone followed him—a living person. There might be more, but we don't have time to watch the whole thing."

Not with Alissa potentially missing. I'd thought she was with Samuel at the time. Safe. No ghost could knock down a vampire, but with dark magic involved, all bets were off. In a town this small, there were only so many places she might have disappeared to, but how long did we have to find her before it was too late?

Nathan's expression darkened. "I'll help you look for her. Let me tell Steve first."

As he moved over to the gargoyles, I went outside to waylay Maura. She was still glued to the camera screen, with Carey peering over her shoulder. My dad waited on the other side of the door.

"Sorry, this looks like complete madness," I said to him. "I don't know that the police are going to be much help, but if someone *did* take Alissa, then I have no idea whereabouts they are."

"I can track people—non-ghosts, I mean," Maura offered. "I don't know that I'm familiar enough with your friend to be able to do it, but I can try."

"You can… track her? Without a tracking spell?"

"Yeah, but it's not a skill I'm in the habit of frequently using," she said. "Blair, relax. The ghost—whoever it really is—is trying to mess with your head."

"At least two people are dead because of them," I reminded her. "Besides, I can hardly turn my back. Even my living room isn't safe from planks of wood flying through the window."

Maura tilted her head. "You know, it makes way more sense for that to have been a living person who threw that plank of wood rather than a ghost."

"I'm not sure Alissa would appreciate the distinction at the moment."

On the other hand, it wasn't a ghost we were looking for but a witch. Ghosts were Maura's expertise, but if dark magic was truly behind this, then I knew exactly who to ask for guidance.

"Then I'll track her down," Maura said.

"Not yet." I turned to my dad. "I need to figure out what we're up against, first of all. I have to talk to someone who knows all about dark magic. That means it's time to come clean to Madame Grey."

14

With my dad at my side, I entered the witches' headquarters and searched for Madame Grey. While she might have gone home by this hour if she had heard about the incident at the hospital, she might still be at work if she hadn't.

My guess turned out to be on the mark, as she answered when I knocked on the door. "Come in."

I pushed open the door and walked in, while my dad opted to wait outside.

Madame Grey's brows rose when she saw me. "Blair. I heard about some incident involving my granddaughter and that she lost her phone. I assume you've come to explain?"

I hadn't intended to be the one to deliver the bad news myself, but it threw me that she'd been completely oblivious to everything going on. The witch council must be keeping her busy. "It's been a really long week, but the short story is that someone in town is using dark magic, and I think they took Alissa."

I gave her a rundown of my ghost-hunting misadventures that week. She acted utterly unsurprised to learn there'd been a Reaper in town all week, though her attention sharpened when I detailed the incident at the hospital and the plank of wood sailing through our window.

"We couldn't figure out how a ghost could possibly be that strong," I said to her. "I should have come and told you right away, but we went to report it to the police first. Alissa told me she'd handle the report while I went with Maura to talk to the last ghost hunter who came to town. He was called Leroy Quint. Since he died in Sloan last weekend, nobody realised he was magical at first."

"You were present when he died?" She pinched the bridge of her nose. "You have a knack for walking into these situations, don't you?"

"I was with my foster parents in Sloan when I saw him," I explained. "Everyone thought his death was a weird accident, but I didn't realise he'd been to Fairy Falls until Nathan looked him up, and I found out he was a ghost hunter."

"So you assumed he came to seek out this Shadow on the Lake too?"

"Exactly," I said. "After the ghost started to get violent, Maura decided to talk to him in person. He told us his own experience of the ghost, and she also found the footage on the camera he dropped at the scene. But then I got a message from Alissa…"

I showed her my phone screen, and her eyes narrowed. "Didn't her phone go missing?"

"Yeah, after the hospital incident." I closed the message. "For that reason, I'm not sure if they actually have her or if it's a bluff, but she isn't at home. She left the police station with Samuel while I was gone, but I would have thought her next stop would be here."

"I agree, Blair," she said. "But who, exactly, is responsible for this?"

"I honestly don't know," I admitted. "We spent so long assuming it was a ghost we were after, but while there *is* some kind of ghostly creature on the loose at the lake, I don't know if it's her who killed those two ghost hunters. Also, we found another ghost at the lake on our first trip there, a teenage witch called Mattie Lyons."

Madame Grey sucked in a breath. "I remember her disappearance."

"You do?" I should have known, and I wished I'd brought Maura straight to her from the start. "She's been trying to warn us away from the Shadow on the Lake all week. She said the ghost would hurt everyone we cared about... but if it's not the ghost, then who was she warning us against?"

"Her former coven," Madame Grey murmured. "Some of them must have survived."

My heart missed a beat. "What coven?"

"They were called the Yarrow Coven," she said. "They were forcibly disbanded when it was discovered that they were dabbling in dangerous magic."

"Dangerous magic? Like… like rituals?"

"I thought we caught them before they could do anything irreversible," said Madame Grey. "There were a number of nasty incidents connected to their coven but nothing we could conclusively prove was their work. Mattie's disappearance was what ultimately led me to shut them down, but it wasn't a popular idea. The coven was almost entirely comprised of young witches with no family or birth coven."

"I think I know what you mean," I said quietly. "There's… there's this girl at the police station right now, from Fairfield House. I think she might be one of them, but she's just a kid."

"I see." Her expression was grave. "The police weren't fussed about wasting their resources on a group of half-wild children, and since I was never able to find out who was their leader, they couldn't make any arrests. I hardly wanted to ruin the prospects of young witches who'd already fallen through the cracks, so I let it go."

"What about Mattie, though?" I asked. "Some of them must have known what happened to her."

"The police questioned some of them, but none of them admitted to knowing anything," she said. "We assumed she drowned while swimming in the lake, and her friends were too frightened of getting into trouble to admit they'd led her into danger. The police dropped the case, but I did manage to recruit some of the former Yarrow Coven members to join the Meadowsweet Coven."

"Good," I said. "There can't be that many of them out there, unless they've been recruiting."

"They might well have been." Her expression shadowed. "And now they've taken my granddaughter."

"Either that or Samuel took her to his home so they could hide out until the madness is over," I said. "They can't have taken him, too, right? If it's really a bunch of kids doing this, they can't be a match for a vampire."

"I wouldn't underestimate them," Madame Grey said. "When I was looking into the sort of magic they were doing, I found out they'd been experimenting with spells to enhance their own capabilities by... well, by draining the life force of another person."

My mouth went dry. "What do you mean?"

"One of the witches in the coven made herself strong enough to lift a car, but the effort involved severely hurting the other person she was taking energy from. Ritual magic always has a cost."

Ritual magic. I'd seen it up close before. Around a year ago, a local wizard had attempted to gain the abilities of other types of paranormals by sacrificing them in a ritual intended to transfer their powers to him. The sort of witches and wizards who dabbled in ritual magic tended to have no qualms about transferring that cost onto other people.

"So someone could make themselves strong enough to rip off a fence panel and throw it through a window?" It didn't explain why we hadn't seen the intruder, but we hadn't been looking out the window at the time, and they might have stood out of sight. "What about pulling Alissa out the window, then?"

"It might have been a simple levitating spell cast from someone hiding near the scene," said Madame Grey. "The same as the spell that pulled you into the lake."

"A levitation spell?" Heat rushed to my face at the notion that it'd been a child with a wand who'd thrown me into the lake, not a terrifying ghost. "She got Carey, too, but if Maura hadn't grabbed her, she might have drowned."

"Precisely," said Madame Grey. "These witches are incredibly dangerous, and I intend to make it clear to the police that they should prioritise this case."

"Good." When she stood up, I added, "Steve wouldn't listen to us, but there are at least two deaths that can be linked back to this coven. Three if you count Mattie."

"Precisely." She stepped out from behind her desk. "Shall we be off?"

Outside the office, my dad waited beside the door. "Madame Grey. I've offered to help Blair find your granddaughter if there's anything I can do to help."

"I'm grateful for your efforts, Mr Clearwater," Madame Grey said. "I've been kept busy by those bickering council members all week, but I have a few matters I intended to discuss with you. Once my granddaughter is safe, of course."

"I look forward to it." Dad fell into step with me, while Madame Grey strode through the lobby and overtook both of us in seconds. He leaned closer to me. "I heard most of what you discussed. What do you want to do next?"

"Maura claimed that she might be able to use her Reaper skills to track Alissa, but there's no guarantee," I replied. "Given that her kidnappers have her phone, I can try calling her and see where it leads me."

"Then you run the risk of walking into a trap," he said. "You don't know how many coven members will be waiting for you. I'll wake some of the fairies and ask if any of them are willing to help. I'm sure they'll gladly back you up."

"I don't..." I trailed off. "I don't want anyone to get hurt."

"You've done so much for all of us," he said. "Let us do something for you in return."

"All right, but we should check with Madame Grey

first." I quickened my pace to catch up to the coven leader. "Before we go looking, should I call Alissa's number and see what happens?"

"It certainly can't hurt at this stage," replied Madame Grey.

I opened her message and hit the call back button, but it went straight to voicemail. Either they'd taken precautions or Alissa no longer had her phone. Worth a try.

Worry fluttering in my chest, I hit reply instead. *Tell me where she is. What do you want me to do?*

They couldn't possibly know that the fairies and Madame Grey might be ready to back me up as well as Maura. And however many people were left in the Yarrow Coven, we ought to be able to beat them with sheer numbers regardless of whatever dark magic they'd accessed. I hoped.

A response came almost at once. *Come to the lake alone. Or she dies.*

My heart leapt into my throat, and I looked up at Madame Grey. "They replied, whoever has Alissa. They want me to go to the lake, and if I don't go alone, they'll kill her."

"They wouldn't dare." Madame Grey marched ahead towards the police station, while Dad gave my shoulder a reassuring squeeze.

"I'll be back soon," he said. He vanished in a flutter of wings.

Up ahead, Maura watched Madame Grey enter the police station with one eyebrow raised. "That's her?" She approached me. "The coven leader?"

"That's Madame Grey, yes." I drew in a breath. "She helped me figure out that the witches who took Alissa were part of a coven that was forcibly shut down for dabbling in dark magic a few years ago. I think they summoned the Shadow on the Lake initially. Mattie was one of them. They were called the Yarrow Coven."

Her eyes widened. "They were shut down… but they survived?"

"Apparently so," I said. "At a guess, they don't want us exposing their crimes. According to the message one of them just sent me, I have to meet them alone by the lake, or they'll kill Alissa."

"Then where's Madame Grey going?"

"To talk Steve into taking this seriously," I answered. "My dad's going to see if any of the fairies are willing to back us up, since we don't know how many people we're up against—but if I don't go to meet them alone, I risk Alissa's life."

"Then go alone," Maura said. "If I use my Reaper powers to stay hidden, they won't know I'm there."

"You'd better be right." I couldn't deny that her particular brand of chaos might be just what we needed, and I doubted this mismatched former coven had expected to have to deal with a Reaper.

I went into the police station to fetch Nathan while Madame Grey confronted Steve. If not for my lingering worry over Alissa, it might have been amusing to hear her giving him a piece of her mind. Nathan came with me at once, and when I told him about Alissa's message, his expression turned grim.

"I won't let you go completely alone," he told me. "Those of us who plan to confront the coven will find somewhere to watch you from nearby, so we'll be ready to step in if need be."

"All right." We didn't have any time to waste on arguments, so I nodded. "We'll go to the lake via the forest path, so my dad can meet us on the way. That okay?"

"Sure." He stepped aside when Madame Grey emerged from the police station. "Madame Grey, Blair needs to meet the coven alone."

"She told me," Madame Grey said. "I've already contacted several witches and told them to join you near the lake."

"Tell them to keep their distance." I beckoned to Maura. "I'd tell Carey to wait with Madame Grey if you want to come with me. Nathan and I are heading to the lake now."

Carey made a noise of protest, but I was already walking away, urgency building with every step. Each second that passed risked Alissa's fate becoming irreversible, and I'd rather face the coven while outnumbered than let her die.

I hadn't taken two steps into the forest before I spotted my dad approaching, accompanied by several other fairies. Sky came bounding up to join me, and I gave him a stroke. "So you decided to wake up, did you?"

"Take him with you," Dad said. "If they want to meet you alone, they won't count your familiar as an extra person."

"Miaow," Sky said, his tone disgruntled.

"Hey, it's a good thing if they underestimate you," I reassured him. Familiars were often viewed as more of an extension of their witch, like a wand, but the coven would never guess what secrets Sky was hiding.

I just hoped it'd be enough.

"Ready?" Maura stepped onto the path behind me. "I

convinced Carey to stay with the witches. Are all these fairies really coming with us?"

"Of course," Dad said.

Ani stepped to the front of their group. "We're with you."

Warmth filled my chest. "I appreciate it, but the coven is expecting me to meet them alone. If you go down the path that comes out near the waterfall, then you should be able to approach them from behind. I doubt they're expecting glamour."

"Good idea," Dad said. "I'll lead the way."

After we parted ways with the fairies, Maura, Nathan, and I continued to follow the path towards the lake. I had to keep reminding both of them to stay far enough back to give the illusion that I was on my own.

When the lake came into view, however, it was pretty clear that nobody was waiting for me on the shore. Living or dead. Had the witches known I wouldn't come alone, or had it all been a bluff?

I peered through the trees. "I can't see anyone. Can you?"

"I'm going to talk to Mattie again," Maura said. "See if she knows."

"All right."

Nathan swore under his breath when Maura called the darkness to her hands, seeming to siphon from the shadows beneath the trees. "Mattie, are you there?"

"What now?" Mattie's ghost appeared in front of us, her arms folded across her chest. "How many times do I have to tell you to leave me alone?"

"Did your ex-coven kill you?" asked Maura. "The Yarrow Coven? Does that name mean anything to you?"

"So you didn't keep your word," said another voice from near the lake.

Mattie vanished into the shadows while I hurried forwards, looking for the speaker. Several figures appeared from the surrounding trees, gathering on the path. The Yarrow Coven had showed up after all.

The first thing I noticed was that they didn't have Alissa with them. Or Samuel either. All were female, and all but one looked to be teenagers.

The sole exception was Evana, the elderly witch we'd spoken to earlier. Evana *Yarrow*. She must be their leader, and she'd been hiding in plain sight the whole time.

"Neither did you." I walked out of the forest to face the newcomers, Sky padding alongside me. "Where is Alissa?"

"She'll stay safe as long as you cooperate with us," said Evana.

I didn't move. "How long have you been hiding for? Has the Yarrow Coven stayed intact the whole time?"

"Hiding?" She laughed. "I didn't need to hide, since nobody was looking for me."

I clenched my hands at my sides. "Until you killed too many people who came close to guessing the truth."

Her expression hardened. "There are some things that aren't worth stirring up."

"But using illegal magical rituals is perfectly safe, is it?"

She laughed again. "I suppose the Meadowsweet Coven has warped your sense of morality when it comes to magic. Your friend is the sort of witch I have no patience with. Set on controlling the limits of magic, judgmental of anyone forced to turn to other methods to survive..."

"You're the one who recruited a bunch of teenagers

who were desperate." I indicated her companions. "You can't pretend there was no manipulation involved."

"I gave them an offer they were glad to accept," she retaliated. "No other coven would have taken them in."

"That isn't true. Madame Grey would have been willing to give anyone a second chance." I looked defiantly at her. "And no coven at all is better than one that delights in hurting people. Who did you convince to throw that plank of wood at us? Who killed Leroy Quint or caused the author of that article to crash his car? Or did you do most of that yourself?"

A couple of the teenage witches exchanged guilty looks, but nobody spoke. Evana tutted. "It's a pity you had to fall in with those Meadowsweet Witches. You're an outsider, and someone to shake up the covens is just what Fairy Falls needs."

"You can't ply me with compliments," I said. "Not when you killed at least two people—not including Mattie. Or was it the so-called Shadow on the Lake who killed her?"

"It was an accident," one of the teenage witches blurted. "Mattie wasn't supposed to die."

"What does that mean, exactly?" I asked.

"She volunteered." The teenage witch flinched when Evana shot her a warning look, but I gave her an encouraging nod, and she kept speaking. "We were trying… we were trying to use a ritual to contact the dead. Mattie was right at the centre. She wanted to find her family, who died when she was a kid, but it went wrong."

"How?" I asked.

"Something else showed up," whispered one of the other teenage witches. "And it killed her."

"A ghoul, to be precise." Maura appeared from the shadows at my side, causing the group of teenage witches to jump back in alarm. "You thought a dark-magic ritual would bring back a normal ghost, but you got a ghoul instead and let it stick around for years, attacking anyone who got close to the lake."

A ghoul? I'd never heard of one of those before, so I'd have to take Maura's word for it.

"You shouldn't be here, Reaper," Evana warned Maura.

"I'd like to see you keep a Reaper from hunting down ghosts," she replied. "Imagine my disappointment when it turned out to be a bunch of cowardly witches behind all this."

They were less scary now we could see all of them and they were no longer hiding behind a ghost, but what had they done with Alissa? And where was Samuel?

"I've had enough of this." Evana pulled out her wand.

The teenage witches hesitated, but one by one, they all did the same.

Sky leapt forward and transformed into his giant monstrous form, positioning himself in front of Maura and me. "*Miaow.*"

All the witches except for Evana fled, shrieking about monsters, while Maura vanished into the shadows. Evana pointed her wand at me, but I snapped my fingers and brought out my fairy wings, taking flight out of range of her spell. Sky advanced on Evana, growling, a heartbeat before Maura reappeared behind the fleeing witches.

The witches scattered, shrieking, but even Maura's Reaper skills didn't seem to faze Evana. She aimed her wand at me again, so I snapped my fingers to glamour myself unseen before flitting behind and aiming my wand at her back.

I wasn't the only one. Several other fairies appeared alongside me, casting their own spells. In seconds, ropes bound Evana's hands and feet, while the teenage witches cowered away from Sky's monstrous form.

"Where is she?" I snapped my fingers to reappear and approached Evana. "Where is Alissa?"

"She's in the Shadow on the Lake's home," she told me. "So is the vampire."

Samuel. I hadn't told her about him, so she must be telling the truth.

Alissa and Samuel were trapped with the ghoul.

15

We might have managed to trap the Yarrow Coven, including their leader, but if Alissa was in the grip of the Shadow on the Lake, then this was far from over.

"She's in the Shadow on the Lake's home?" Maura addressed Evana and the rest of her coven. "Whereabouts does it live, exactly?"

"An island in the middle of the lake." It was Mattie who answered, to my astonishment, her ghost emerging from the bushes at the edge of the path. "You'd better move fast if you want to save her."

She drifted away from the captive witches, beckoning us down the path circling the lake.

I didn't move. "Why are you helping us?"

"Does it matter?" She drifted farther down the path. "Follow me. I'll show you."

My lie-sensing powers hadn't picked up on any untruths in the witches' explanation, but ghosts could lie. Could I really trust her?

"Come on." She beckoned again. "The Shadow on the Lake usually comes ashore to feed, but with prey already in its nest, it won't need to."

My stomach lurched. "Is that why it always appears around midnight?"

"Blair?" Nathan trod past the captive witches, not seeing Mattie hovering above the lake. "Do you know where Alissa is?"

"An island in the middle of the lake, allegedly," I replied. "The Shadow on the Lake's lair, in fact. Mattie claims she can take us there, but it might be a trap."

"I thought the stories didn't turn out to be real." His gaze travelled over the lake, passing straight through Mattie's transparent form.

"The Shadow on the Lake is real, but those witches had no idea what it really was," I explained. "According to Maura, it's a ghoul."

"Come *on*." Mattie beckoned to me again. "Do you want your friend to still be inside the nest when it wakes up?"

"I'll tell Madame Grey," said Nathan. "She'll be on her way now, I expect. Can Maura get rid of this ghost?"

"Yes," Maura answered. "I'm going with Mattie. Searching the whole lake on foot will take too long, and it doesn't sound like your friend has that much time."

"Exactly." I didn't dare risk Alissa's life. "Make sure those witches don't get away. I'll be right back."

"Blair—be careful." Nathan watched, concern etched on his face, as Maura and I hurried after Mattie's transparent figure. I still didn't fully trust her not to lead us straight into a trap, but Maura was right—the sheer size of the lake made it impossible to search every inch of the place before midnight struck, especially in the darkness.

We walked south until we left the boundaries of the town behind. Mattie drifted alongside us, the lake a sheet of obsidian on our left-hand side. I didn't see any islands on the water, but the dark expanse was vast enough to hide any number of secrets.

"What's a ghoul, exactly?" I asked Maura.

"Corrupted spirits that feed on human flesh," she replied. "Nasty creatures. They tend to show up when a ritual goes wrong, and it sounds like this one did. Majorly. It sounds like the sort of unpleasant sacrificial ritual that the ex-coven leader in Hawkwood Hollow would have tried to cover up to save her own reputation. I can't say her coven ever let a creature like that loose for *that* long, though."

My throat closed up. "Feed on human flesh? You might have mentioned that earlier."

"I didn't want to freak you out. Besides, they sleep during the day."

"It's not day." Alissa had hours left at most. "You'd think a flesh-eating monster living in the middle of the lake would draw attention from the merpeople and the other inhabitants."

"Not if it spends most of the time sleeping," Maura said.

"We did the ritual on an island on the eastern edge where nobody lives," Mattie added. "The Shadow on the Lake stayed and made the island into its home."

"How *did* Evana and her teenage minions manage to get Alissa and Samuel onto the island?" I asked. "I know they probably took Alissa's wand away, but Samuel is a vampire. He ought to have been able to outrun them."

"Vamps aren't known for being great swimmers," Maura commented. "In fact, they can't cross running water at all. Not sure if a lake counts, but if there's no way off the island anyway…"

"Then it probably doesn't matter." I turned to Mattie. "Evana left the pair of them as bait, didn't she? You might have told me it was the witches and not the Shadow on the Lake who were trying to attack my friends."

"I'm helping you now, aren't I?"

"You'd better be," said Maura. "No funny business, is that clear?"

Mattie scoffed and didn't answer. In spite of it all, I didn't think she was out to manipulate us. She was still a kid, really, and her life had been sacrificed to summon the ghoul in the first place. Then her fellow coven members had abandoned her and fled, leaving her death unsolved and her grave neglected.

Yet the spectre of the Shadow on the Lake had remained, and so had Evana. She must have stayed in contact with the surviving coven members to ensure that nobody else ever found out the truth of what had happened that night.

"There it is." Mattie pointed towards the eastern edge of the lake, where a darker blur on the surface hinted at a solid landmass. "See that island?"

Maura stopped walking. "Yes, I do."

"Unless you have a boat hidden somewhere, then how are you planning to get there?" I asked her. "I have wings, but you don't. Also, wings won't stop that thing from yanking me into the lake again."

"I can walk through the shadows, remember?" she replied. "Not only that, but I can take you with me."

That didn't sound appealing in the slightest. "I didn't know you could take normal people along for the ride."

"I can, but I won't pretend it'll be a pleasant experience," she said. "Also, when I shortcut to a new location, I'm more or less going in blindfolded. I won't know if we're about to land on top of that creature until we're already on the island."

"You're not doing much to convince me, you know."

"I'm making it clear that once you take that step, there's no going back," Maura told me. "It's your choice."

Was there really a choice? I needed to get to Alissa, and if the quickest and safest route was through the shadows, so be it. "All right."

Darkness folded around Maura's entire body. "Grab my arm, and if you don't want to get stuck in the afterworld, don't let go of me."

Well. That was certainly an incentive to take this seriously. I reached out a hand, and she grabbed my wrist and yanked me into the darkness.

Shadows engulfed us on all sides in a cold and suffocating embrace. I'd barely begun to take in the sheer discomfort and terror before the shadows spat us out above a narrow strip of land in the middle of the lake.

Alissa and Samuel both jumped when we appeared next to them. Recovering, Samuel lunged forward with dizzying vampire speed, fangs bared.

"It's only me!" I held up my hands, but he flew straight past me and would have crashed into Maura if she hadn't vanished into the shadows.

Samuel caught himself an instant before he fell into

the water, while Maura reappeared behind a stunned Alissa.

"Blair...?" Alissa said faintly. "Samuel—what are you doing?"

"You," Samuel growled at Maura. "You're responsible for this, Reaper. You could have got us killed."

"She brought me here to help you," I said hastily. "We need to get out of here. Finish your argument when we're back on solid ground."

"Exactly," said Maura. "Did you know this is the island where the Yarrow Coven initially did the ritual to summon the Shadow on the Lake? If you want to stay here until it wakes up, then it's your choice, but I think your girlfriend would rather come with me."

"Yes. She would." Alissa shuddered.

Samuel gave Maura a derisive look. "How exactly did you plan to get us off the island?"

"Good question." I turned to her. "I don't think Maura can carry all three of us through the afterworld at once... or can you?"

Samuel gave me a flat stare. "Frankly, I would rather drown."

Oh boy. I should have seen that one coming.

"Blair can fly you out instead then," Maura said to him.

"No, I can't," I said. "My wings aren't strong enough to support more than one person. We should have brought a boat."

Granted, a boat was no safer than the island itself, not when the Shadow on the Lake was as dangerous in the water as outside of it.

"Vampires do not ride in boats," Samuel informed me.

"Beggars can't be choosers when you're stuck on an

island where a ritualistic murder took place," said Maura. "Where's the creature's nest, anyway?"

Samuel bared his fangs at her in answer.

"Stop it," Alissa protested. "I'm willing to endure a little discomfort to get out of here before that thing wakes up. I think that mess of branches over there is its nest."

"Branches?" Maura took a step in the direction she'd pointed in. "I don't sense anything… wait."

A chill brushed against my back, and a dark shape appeared above the water on our right-hand side. *Oh no.*

The ghoul looked even less like a person up close, with long, drooping limbs and a wide mouth brimming with sharp-looking teeth.

Maura tensed, shadows filling her hands. "Stay back."

Alissa took a step back, the colour draining from her face, while Samuel stared at the creature with wide eyes. Could his fangs even make a dent in that creature? I certainly wouldn't have wanted to sink my teeth into it, but I had to do something. I reached into my pocket for my wand.

"You can't hurt it," Maura whispered to me. "Divert its attention, and I'll do the rest."

I was all too happy to get out of the line of fire, but Alissa and Samuel didn't have wings, and there was nowhere for them to run.

I'd have to distract it instead. Snapping my fingers, I vanished in a flash of glitter. The bright flare drew the ghoul's attention, and I reappeared, flitting above the water.

One of the creature's limbs extended like a long tentacle, grabbing hold of my legs. I yelped and flailed, waving my wand, but I only succeeded in making it rain glitter. "Maura, a little help would be nice."

Maura's shadowy form grabbed at the creature, but it refused to relinquish its hold on me. Alarm blared through me as the beast drew me closer to its gaping mouth. *Think, Blair.*

The video footage had shown the ghost hunter using magic to defend himself, and he'd managed to break the ghoul's hold using some kind of bright flash. I hadn't seen exactly what he'd done, but perhaps the beast avoided the daylight for a reason.

Squeezing my eyes shut, I cast a blinding spell.

The creature's grip released me at once. I flew high, out of range, and opened my eyes as Maura seized the ghoul's tentacles from behind. Shadows flooded the area, and the outline of what appeared to be a door appeared in the gloom. For a moment, I wondered if my eyes were playing tricks on me, but Maura tugged on the ghoul's limbs to drag it through the door, but it held on tenaciously. Gritting her teeth, she snarled, "It's no use fighting me, ghoul."

I waved my wand and cast another flash of blinding light. The beast shrank away, and Maura gained the upper hand. Wrestling the beast halfway through the door, she gave a firm shove.

The darkness behind the door drew the ghoul into its embrace, and in another blink, it was gone. The ghoul, the shadows, and the creepy door all vanished at the same time.

"What was that?" I gestured vaguely towards the spot where the door had appeared.

"The afterworld... the real one." Maura grimaced,

rubbing her arms. "I didn't count on it being that cumbersome to grab."

"Maybe you ought to invest in a scythe if you make a habit of that kind of thing," I said.

"I tried to borrow one," she said. "The Reaper Council objects to non-members using their props without permission."

On second thought, maybe Maura running around with a scythe was not something anyone needed to deal with. She had more than enough skills of her own.

"Is it gone?" Alissa asked, holding on to Samuel's arm.

"Yes," said Maura. "Also, I've just figured out how you can get back to shore without taking a trip through the afterworld. Follow me."

She sank into the lake, and the waters parted to either side of her as if pushed outward by an invisible force. A shadowy path formed behind her, leading up to the bank of the island.

Samuel didn't budge. "I am *not* walking on that."

"Feel free to spend the night here if you'd prefer," Maura said over her shoulder. "If not, follow me. The path will disappear as soon as I leave. Fair warning."

"I'll go first," I told Alissa and Samuel. "Trust me, you'd rather do it this way than take a shortcut through the shadows."

I flew downward and landed on the path, which was solid enough to walk on despite the unnatural way it cut through the water, the lake rippling on either side.

After a moment's hesitation, Alissa followed me. "This isn't so bad. Come on, Samuel."

I waited for her to coax Samuel off the island, though I could have flown if I wanted to. But I didn't want to let

Alissa out of my sight after her narrow escape, and eventually, Samuel caved in and followed her onto the path Maura carved through the water.

When we touched down on the shore, the path vanished, the lake returning to its pristine state. Mattie's ghost drifted over to meet us. "You did it."

"The Shadow on the Lake has gone," Maura said. "I can help you move on, too, if you like. Want me to do that?"

Her gaze travelled over the lake to the spot where the remnants of the Yarrow Coven were restrained. "Yes, please."

Darkness clouded Maura's hands. A moment later, Mattie's ghost vanished.

"Did you send her through to the next world?" I asked. "I didn't see the door this time."

"Normally, non-Reapers can't see any of this," she said. "That ghoul was freakishly strong. It took all my strength to wrestle that thing through the door."

"And it won't find Mattie?" I asked.

"No." She shook her head. "Whatever awaits on the other side, she's at peace now. That thing won't bother her again."

It seemed even Reapers didn't know what lay on the other side of death. Perhaps only the dead themselves had the answers to that question. "I hope she's happy now, wherever she is."

With Maura in the lead, the four of us circled the lake back to the place where we'd left the remnants of the Yarrow Coven.

By this point, they were surrounded by a combination of gargoyle shifters, witches, and fairies. Upon spotting Madame Grey, Alissa ran to meet her grandmother, accompanied by Samuel. Among the fairies, my dad gave me an approving nod, while Nathan came to embrace me.

Sky wrapped himself around my legs, purring. "Miaow."

"Hey." I hugged Nathan back then released him. "Is Steve here yet?"

"He's on his way," he answered. "Evana will face consequences for what she did."

"Good." The kids, though… Evana had manipulated them. They wouldn't get away without punishment, but they deserved the chance to start afresh. Make better choices.

Madame Grey would give them that, I was sure. For Mattie's sake.

16

Maura left town the following morning before I went to work.

"That could have gone worse" was her overall verdict on the week's events after I walked with her to the border of town to see her off.

"It could also have gone better," I said. "I have a broken window and fence to fix once I get home from work."

"True, but at least that Evana got caught after all these years," she said. "She deserves to rot behind bars for what she did to those kids."

"Yeah." She did. As expected, Madame Grey had reached out to the children Evana had recruited in an attempt to mitigate the damage, though the girl from Fairfield House who'd sent us to see Evana was a trouble-maker if I ever saw one. At least Mattie's ghost had been laid to rest, and the ghoul was no longer a threat. "I forgot to ask… did you actually manage to get any video footage for Carey's blog in the end?"

"Some," Carey answered. "Obviously, I didn't see anything that happened on the island, but I got some creepy footage of you being thrown into the water."

"Just leave out the part where it turned out to be a witch who did it," Maura advised her. "We can post a bit of the footage from Leroy Quint's camera, too, if his family gives us permission."

"I'm not sure they'd go for that, to tell you the truth." At least the poor guy's death had been resolved. Evana had admitted to sending one of her young minions with a cursed object after him. It caused him to drop dead, and they buried the evidence afterwards. She hadn't yet confessed to all the crimes she'd committed over the years, but she had a long jail sentence awaiting her.

"Worth a shot." Maura nodded to Carey. "All right, we'd better move."

"Good luck," I told them. "And thanks for getting rid of that ghoul."

"Anytime," said Maura. "If you ever find yourselves in need of a Reaper, you know who to call."

"You'd be better off calling the Ghostbusters." Mart snickered in the background.

"Oi," said Maura. "Don't forget you're stuck with me for life. Or afterlife, as it were."

"I never asked," I said. "How did he end up following you around? Even the ghoul was tied to a single place."

"We're both Reapers," she replied. "He's bound to me instead of a place, and it's because of him that I left the Reapers to begin with. They tend to get twitchy when we bring ghosts back instead of banishing them, but I'd rather have my brother than the support of the Reaper Council."

I blinked in surprise. Maura had no shortage of secrets, but I was hardly one to talk. "I'd better head to work anyway. Have a safe flight home."

"Bye." Carey waved at me before mounting her broom, and Maura did the same.

The two of them took flight, Mart's ghost pursuing them into the sky. I watched for a moment before turning back to Fairy Falls. The lake looked deceptively peaceful, its surface reflecting the cloudy sky. Not a ghost to be seen. I briefly regretted not asking Maura a few more questions about the afterworld, though if Maura had to deal with monsters like that ghoul on a regular basis, then it was probably for the best that she hadn't stayed any longer.

In any case, I'd saved Alissa, the witches responsible for summoning it would be jailed, and my foster parents were no longer in danger of any hauntings—from the living or the dead.

———

It was kind of surreal to go back to the office after the excitement of the previous night, but working in paranormal recruitment was never dull. Between Samuel checking in to thank me for sending him his new assistant and a refreshing lack of interruptions from ghosts, the day passed quickly.

After work, I dropped by the witches' headquarters despite not having a magic lesson scheduled. I wanted to check in with Madame Grey about the witches who'd been arrested, preferably without setting eyes on Steve, so I knocked on the door to her office.

"Come in," Madame Grey called from the other side of the door.

I entered her office and almost jumped out of my skin when I found Vincent the vampire standing beside her desk. "Ah… hi, Vincent."

Were they discussing Maura or yesterday's incident? I had no doubt Vincent already knew everything, but I doubted he'd be thrilled that Maura had ended up being the hero of the previous night.

"Am I to understand that the Reaper has left town?" he asked me. "If so, then I'm glad of it."

"Yes, but you already knew that," I replied. "She isn't that bad. We'd have been screwed if she hadn't been there last night."

"I am aware," he said. "I'm glad the outcome was favourable and that Samuel and your friend escaped unscathed. As for that coven, I generally find that anything you try to bury tries to rise to the surface eventually."

Given that he slept in a coffin, I supposed he was the expert, but I was inclined to agree with him. Fairy Falls sat on a ton of secrets, but all it took was an intrepid mind and a big enough shovel. And sometimes a Reaper.

"I will see you later, Blair." He vanished through the door in a blink without waiting for my reply.

"Vampires," I muttered. "I take it he wanted to know if the witches responsible for summoning that ghoul were arrested?"

"Among other things," Madame Grey said. "Evana was found unequivocally guilty of a number of crimes and has been sentenced to jail for life. She might even be transferred to the LPFP if the council agrees on it."

"Good." I hesitated, recalling my last visit to her office. "Um... I know I probably should have told you about Maura being a Reaper from the start. She wanted to keep it quiet..."

"That was her choice, Blair, not yours," she said. "I spoke to her yesterday after the incident by the lake, and we came to an understanding that she'll inform me the next time she visits Fairy Falls."

"Oh, good." It probably didn't hurt that Maura had saved Alissa's life, of course, despite her antics drawing the attention of the ghoul and the coven in the first place. "Ah—what about those teenage witches? Are they in jail too?"

"They're all minors, so they were placed on probation instead," she said. "Under supervision."

"Oh. Good." I sought the right words. "I don't think they should get off without punishment, but if they end up losing their futures because they did as Evana told them, it'll only prove Evana right when she claimed that no coven would ever take them in."

"I'm aware of that, Blair," she said. "If they behave themselves, then I intend to offer them membership in my own coven."

"Really?" Relief spread through me. "I know you have your hands full with the witch council and appeasing the paranormal hunters..."

"I can spare the time to help a group of unfortunate young witches, Blair," she said. "Also, I arranged for your broken window to be repaired."

"Oh, thanks." How did she find the time to handle everyone else's problems? I could barely even remember to put my socks on the right way around, but there was a reason I wasn't a coven leader, after all. "For everything."

After I left her office, I went straight home. True to her word, Madame Grey had already fixed the window. Upon entering the flat, I found Alissa and the cats on the sofa, which was entirely free of wood splinters and broken glass.

"Hey, Blair," Alissa said. "Please tell me your Reaper friend went home."

"She already left this morning. Why?"

"Because Samuel was going to find her and give her a piece of his mind for drawing the attention of that coven and their mad ghost."

"I thought he already forgave her for that," I said. "Honestly, even Vincent was willing to admit she saved the day."

"You've seen Vincent?"

"He was at Madame Grey's office for some reason," I replied. "She told me she fixed the window…"

"Yeah, she did," Alissa replied. "Samuel was all in favour of dragging me to stay on campus with him until he was certain the trouble was over, but with the Yarrow witches in jail, the odds of someone else throwing a plank of wood at us are low."

"Don't speak too soon. That's my motto," I said, seeing movement on the other side of the window. A closer look showed Nathan approaching the house through the new sheet of glass. "Nathan's here. Maybe Steve let him off early for once."

I left the flat and ran to the doorstep to meet him, where Nathan greeted me with a kiss.

"I see you replaced the window."

"Madame Grey did," I replied. "How's Steve?"

"He's in a good mood, probably because he had the chance to take out his anger on that Evana person."

"Figures," I said. "Want to go for a walk?"

I wanted to get some air after a long day in the office, and since it wasn't raining for once and there were no ghostly demands on my attention, now was the perfect time to take a romantic walk with my boyfriend.

As Nathan and I walked through Fairy Falls, the peaceful sound of the waterfall filled the background until my phone buzzed in my pocket.

"Bet that's my foster parents," I remarked, fishing out my phone. "I called them in a panic yesterday, thinking the ghost—I mean, the coven—would go after them. I still don't know if their weird streak of bad luck was their work or not."

"They're safe now," Nathan reassured me.

"Yeah..." The message asked if I wanted to meet up with them again next weekend. "Maybe I should meet them somewhere other than Sloan."

"Up to you," Nathan said. "Didn't you say that they're used to weird things happening to you?"

"Yeah, but there's a difference between regular weird and... this." I gestured to the town as a whole. "Am I mad for thinking I want to bring my foster parents into this anyway?"

"No," he said. "You want them in your life. I understand."

"Too bad the magical world is set on making that impossible." I smothered a sigh. "I already had to mess with their memories once, and if my life keeps ending up crashing into theirs, then it won't be the last time."

After they'd been forcibly given goblin fruit, which had opened their eyes to the fairies, I'd been all too happy to erase that traumatic experience from their memories, but I couldn't protect them all the time, and now they lived close enough to me that the madness from my life could all too easily spill over into theirs. I couldn't watch them constantly.

Nathan glanced sideways at me. "What do you want to do then?"

I shrugged one shoulder. "Looks like I have two options: either I have to cut them out entirely or find a way to reconcile my two lives. As for what that means..."

I wanted them to know the truth. Some of it, anyway. If I had to call them in a panic to check they weren't being chased by ghosts, I didn't want to have to lie about the danger.

If I made that call, then I'd rather induct them into the magical world slowly, though since I'd lived here for almost a year now, it was a little hard to judge how much the average person could cope with. Ghosts and witches, fairies and vampires, werewolves and shifters, and para-normal hunters—it was overwhelming to have all of that dropped on one's head at once, and even my own abrupt introduction to the world of magic hadn't covered Reapers and other ghostly beasts. I was still learning myself.

Maybe we could learn together.

A meow from behind us signalled Sky's approach, and Nathan and I slowed to let him catch up.

"I think he has a knack for knowing when I need advice," I remarked.

"Miaow," Sky agreed.

"Maybe you should start by introducing them to Sky again," Nathan suggested. "Maybe not his monster form, though…"

"True." I crouched to give Sky a stroke. "They already know I'm a little different, and if I tell them Sky is too, it'll be a start. Then… I don't know. My dad, maybe, since they've met him already."

"See what he thinks," Nathan said. "We can always pay him a visit."

"You want to?" Nathan had worked with the fairies to help restrain the Yarrow Coven yesterday, but there was still a wariness between them that I wasn't sure would ever abate, at least on the fairies' part. Yet I wanted to bring Nathan into that part of my life too. "All right. While we're at it, I think you should offer the fairies a chance to work for the security team."

His brows shot up. "Do you think any of them will want to work in close proximity to Steve?"

"Good point, but some of them… I don't think they're suited to work in an office." Or a university campus. Samuel had his assistant, at least, and the other fairies had been more than a match for the remnants of the Yarrow Coven.

"I'll keep it in mind," he said. "I'll come to see your dad, but I think I should save the sales pitches for later."

"That's fair." We'd take it a step at a time, like everything else, until we made Fairy Falls into a place open to everyone. Maybe even some normals, provided I was careful.

Maybe I'd start by telling my foster parents the story of my mother and father meeting… though my dad might be the best person to tell that story. I'd ask him and see what he thought, and we'd figure it out.

Next time my foster parents visited the magical world, it'd be on my own terms.

ABOUT THE AUTHOR

Elle Adams lives in the middle of England, where she spends most of her time reading an ever-growing mountain of books, planning her next adventure, or writing. Elle's books are humorous mysteries with a paranormal twist, packed with magical mayhem.

She also writes urban and contemporary fantasy novels as Emma L. Adams.

Visit http://www.elleadamsauthor.com/ to find out more about Elle's books.

9 781915 250261